Tell Me There's a Reason

GJ Freeman

"A statue stands in a shaded place.

An angel girl with an upturned face

A name is written on a polished rock.

A broken heart the world forgot".

Martina McBride

This is a work of fiction. Names, characters, places, and incidents either are products of the author's imagination or are used fictitiously. Any resemblance to actual events or locales or persons, living or dead, is entirely coincidental.

Contents

A Proposal 4

Hutchisons Last Stand 33

One Year Later 41

Themis 46

Back To The Fold 51

Briefing 58

On Mission 86

Lyla 96

Street Cleaning 107

Takedown 120

Arham 144

The Promise 146

In the Bunker 151

Air Time 161

Deportation 167

Rethink 184

Respite 188

Start Walking 195

Reconnaissance 201

Separation 211

Extraction 216

Afghanistan 226

Recovery 229

The Villa 233

Adapt. Improvise. Overcome. 239

Marmaris 243

Of Mice and Men 248

Libby 254

Running 262

Ambush 271

Sacha and Christian 286

Washing Up 294

Home 302

A Proposal

"Good morning, Stuart. Coffee? Tea?"

Ames asked for coffee. As he'd entered the suite, his nose had immediately distinguished the suggestion of a puzzling, almost chocolate perfume radiating from the kitchenette. The opulence of Ames' immediate environment was clear evidence that Christian only had the best; combined with that aroma, Ames mused that Christian could sell this place in a heartbeat; it was an estate agents wet dream.

Ames was a reluctant motorist, but the tedious drive here had been necessary; a final meeting requested by Christian. Any coffee, good or bad would be welcome, his throat was dry, and he literally needed perking up. Weary, Ames hoped the visit would be a short one. He had a crossword waiting at home, though not much else.

His host smiled, and in his customary working attire; striped shirt, suit trousers suspended from a pair of wide braces and shiny handmade shoes, ambled towards the kitchen, the transition from thick carpet to tiled surface audible beneath his feet.

Ames cast an eye about the room. The walls were a pure white interrupted by a large central window and decorated with modern intelligently lit art. Ames mused that they were almost certainly originals, expensive and not to his taste.

Apart from the small but efficient open plan kitchen there were doors leading elsewhere, most likely to bedrooms, a bathroom; all told a suite that appeared fully self-contained. Ames took a comfortable seat on the passenger's side of the room's centrepiece, a long, wide antique wooden desk carrying the tools of the stockbroker's trade, laptops, keyboards, drives and monitors. There was no phone, he noted. Just a simple intercom. Nor was there evidence of items of a personal nature, no photos, keepsakes, or souvenirs.

Having exhausted the room, Ames considered the man. Peter Christian, erstwhile father to Eddie and Verity. Twins now thankfully deceased. Their death seemed to have had no effect on the man other than a sense of relief. Up to a point Ames understood that. The Twins had been evil, a duopoly as close to pure evil as he had ever known and having been a copper, Ames had run into a few that deserved the label.

Christian made money, almost as if he had a system for printing it. It was all he did. He rarely left the estate and seemed most content in his top floor apartment with his screens, printouts, and computers.

He returned, handing a mug to Ames, who sniffed appreciatively.

"Now what?"

Ames shifted in his chair, cuddling the coffee. He'd come here today expecting to be released, to be sent back into the retirement he'd been resenting. That was until a year or so ago, when Christian had called with an invitation; the dubious morality of which aside, he couldn't resist.

He was reminded of the first time he'd met with Christian; during, what turned out to be, his final criminal investigation, that of the horrific murder of a toddler, Ellen Hood.

Confronted and appalled by the wickedness of his children; twins, Eddie and Verity, Christian had seemed, even then, to be more troubled by the wider effects of their deed than the immediate consequences to his own family. The Hood's lives had been shattered by Ellen's death, the circumstances of which, even now, still disturbed the battle-hardened former policeman.

Some eighteen months subsequent to the slaying, after the Hood's lives had publicly crumbled, Christian had sought Ames out, explaining that he wanted to help them. He'd described what he'd done for Tom, and then, extrapolating mightily on what could possibly occur because of his intervention, he had carefully asked Ames how he'd felt about the events surrounding Ellen's death; apparently needing to know how it had affected him beyond his duty as a policeman.

Appearing satisfied with his response, or possibly having no other options, Christian cautiously asked Ames to watch over Tom and Sacha with a view to minimising any risk to the couple, whatever form that might take. He had surprised himself by agreeing, though not quite certain what it was he'd agreed to. Ellen's case had gotten under his skin.

Over time, as he'd observed the Hood's being repaired and what they were prepared to go through in memoriam, he'd found himself rooting for them, willing them on, like some little paramilitary police force of his own device.

He'd known what was about to happen to Eddie and Verity and couldn't have cared less other than to advise on how to keep Tom and Sacha out of jail. He counted the end result a success story, the blurred lines between a career upholding the law and what justice should really mean for all parties becoming clearer but at the same time, nebulous. He placated himself with the knowledge that despite years of experience, he'd never been able to reconcile himself to the fact that the scales were stacked against the victims. So, he'd just put a thumb on the side of the angels, restoring balance.

Job done, honour satisfied, he'd assumed he was going back to the sofa and the TV. The question just posed indicated that this, whatever this was, wasn't over.

"Sir?"

"Peter, please." Christian looked over his clasped hands at the man opposite. "When we first spoke, I formed the impression that being a policeman could, at times, frustrate you."

Ames nodded, wondering where this was going. "Perhaps."

"My reasons for setting recent events in motion weren't purely selfish. Or at least if they started out that way that's not how I see things now."

"How so?" Ames was intrigued.

Christian settled back into his chair, steepling his fingers, he continued.

"During your career, what more do you suppose you might have achieved if all of the usual constraints were lifted, didn't exist?"

The question came from nowhere and startled as he was by its sudden presence in the room, Ames had to admit that in one form or another it was a debate he'd had with himself many times over the years.

There had been far too many occasions when he'd been forced into the role of a paralysed spectator; had to watch impotently as perfectly proper investigations were invalidated by underhand manipulation of the legal system, or policy decisions driven by invisible influences.

He'd witnessed thieves, drug dealers, rapists and killers sniggering and giving the finger as they swaggered out of court. Ames had tried numerous times to keep the streets clean, but the broom handle had too many times been cut from his hands. Political expediency, local conditions, deals under the table, a handshake on the golf course.

All this and more had meant the public remained at risk while the legal system congratulated itself over long lunches and fat wallets. The DPP, responsible for prosecutions, was a paper tiger, run by, and largely for, bureaucrats, lawyers, and politicians.

"I'll rephrase that." Said Christian, noting a wary Ames.

"Just for a moment, imagine that an organisation, free of political influence, guided only by morality, and with unlimited funding, were at your disposal".

'That wasn't a rephrase'. Thought Ames. *'That was a pitch.'*

Christian observed doubt cross the policeman's face and spoke quickly to dispel it.

"I'm not terribly good at this Stuart so please forgive me. My motives are pure but my approach, clumsy. I'll try to give you some clarity." Christian paused briefly.

"Numbers are my language Stuart, words aren't easy for me to find, so I shall quote Patrizia Reggiani, former wife of Maurizio, one time head of the Gucci fashion house. Convicted of his murder and jailed, she later declined parole; deciding to remain in prison rather than accepting a condition of her early release, that of getting a job. Wealth and status had meant the world to her you see. She famously said in an interview that, 'It's better to cry in a Rolls Royce than to be happy on a bicycle.' This presupposes that life is all about wealth. What you have rather than what you do." Christian was inert, sombre.

"Formerly, I might have considered my own means in the same terms, but now I believe she was wrong. Those words are flippant, frivolous, illustrating a casual regard for humanity. Wealth should have more purpose than providing a single individual with more comfort than is decent. It bestows a responsibility, something I hadn't considered before. And if properly administered, could serve a more valuable purpose."

His sober delivery lifted, he stood, moved to Ames's side of the desk getting closer for emphasis. Perching on the corner rim he continued.

"The twins were the catalyst, the scales fell from my eyes, if you like, mine was an insulated world." Christian placed an emphasis on *'was.'* "But their atrocity had a ripple effect, something like a stone tossed into calm water, disturbing a hitherto placid existence, destroying an innocent tranquillity and not just that of the victim."

Ames knew exactly who Christian was referring to.

"Being able to set that right, albeit relatively free of the bounds of law, felt as good to me as all this." Christian spread his arms, indicating the trappings of his money-making machine.

"I'd like to do more. I'd be thoroughly bored if I carried on creating wealth and all I did was increase my profits. Numbers are meaningless without purpose. But I don't really know how to do anything else. I'm not made for anything else you see. But you are, and I believe that between us, we can make a difference, no matter how small. I'm offering you that opportunity. Free from influence, financial constrictions, and political interference."

Christian fell silent; aware of the implications of his overture, waiting for a response from Ames.

"You're serious?"

Christian nodded.

"Have you any idea what you're proposing? Where these kinds of good intentions invariably end?"

Christian's brow furrowed. "Frankly, no. I don't. That's why I'm talking to you, with your background and experience I consider you the expert". He paused. "For the time being, if it makes you more comfortable, let's just call this a consultation. But consider some of the other implications". Ames wondered where he was going with this.

"My ex-wife for example. A by-product of our facilitating Mr and Mrs Hood," Ames noted the use of the determiner 'our', implying guilt by association. He considered but rejected the notion that this conversation was any kind of trap. Christian was guileless, if anything naïve; a number crunching innocent abroad and was perhaps simply apportioning accountability, balancing the books. He carried on listening.

"Is that by misappropriating evidence, and supplying the vilest content to her children, she is extremely likely to be struck off for abusing her position. She may even be fortunate to evade a custodial sentence".

Ames reflected just how much Christian was trying to distance himself from what had been his family.

"The media are tearing her apart, just as it should. It's entirely likely she'll never show herself in public again and certainly will no longer be able to interfere with Justice as she so often did in the past."

Ames smiled at that and had to agree. Sometimes it isn't simply criminals that need to be dealt with. Their apologists are often more of a nuisance, unable to be stopped whilst the system is there for them to exploit.

"Is she going to be a problem." Ames felt himself being drawn in.

"It's difficult to say at the moment. My lawyers have dealt with the divorce and its financial implications. I'm free of her. Whether she feels the same about me remains to be seen."

"Do you know where she is now?"

"I do as it happens. My lawyers informed me that they had to amend some of the paperwork due to her reverting back to her maiden name, Hutchison. I'm told that she has moved to Scotland, buying an estate no less, shooting, fishing and the like. I have no idea why. She loathes the countryside."

"Fine." Said Ames. "Let me know if things look like getting out of hand. She never struck me as the, 'go quietly' type of woman".

Christian dismissed the issue with a wave of his hand.

"I've made a start." He said, then paused, noting Ames's startled expression.

"Nothing untoward. I've retained the two principals."

Ames had yet to meet the "two principals" as Christian had put it, James and Ollie, ex SF, now security specialists in the private sector. During his stint watching over Tom and Sacha, they'd become a distant but familiar asset and he'd been quietly impressed at their efficiency and discretion.

"Additionally, on the recommendation of the principals, I've engaged an analyst. Bailey Daniels, a first-class researcher. Meticulous, scrupulous, who I believe is very much on side. That, however, would be for you to judge; history has taught me that my own character assessment abilities are somewhat limited."

Ames reflected briefly on what had been said so far.

"What sort of wrongs are you thinking could be put right?"

"As I said before, that's not up to me Stuart. That's for someone like you to decide. I have the means and some motivation. Beyond that, no knowledge or expertise."

"It's going to cost a lot of money." Ames remarked, absent-mindedly.

"And the means are here, in fact, they're dormant, waiting."

"It'll be some time before anything is achieved. The set up alone may take months."

"Take all the time you need."

Ames had to admit that all his years of policing hadn't given him any of the deep satisfaction he'd felt whilst helping Tom and Sacha. In his time, he'd witnessed a relentless flow of new 'initiatives' issued from on high, that conflicted with genuine, effective, and ethical law enforcement.

Performance Indicators that massaged the crime figures, catch a drunk, charge him, convict him. Score one in the crimes committed v crimes solved column, and much cheaper and easier than finding a murderer. It looked great on PowerPoint, statistically impressive and slick. But it was a stone-cold fact that the system reduced solid, vocational coppers to deskbound, ink stained, form fillers; not a force to be reckoned with. Meanwhile, the public, real people like Tom and Sacha, were abandoned, left isolated, often traumatised, utterly helpless. Victims of real crimes. He'd met them, and despaired.

He'd tried to beat the system from within, but the impotence was too deeply ingrained. The swamp too polluted. In refusing to tug his forelock, Ames had seen his career path skew sideways, and knew that the slide was terminal. He'd long ago acknowledged that he'd be treading water until retirement; sustaining himself in the old fashioned way with Sir Robert Peels 9 policing principles, first set out in 1829. One of them, the fifth, he knew verbatim.

To seek and preserve public favour, not by pandering to public opinion, but by constantly demonstrating absolute impartial service to law, in complete independence of policy, and without regard to the justice or injustice of the substance of individual laws, by ready offering of individual service and friendship to all members of the public without regard to their wealth or social standing, by ready exercise of courtesy and friendly good humour, and by ready offering of individual sacrifice in protecting and preserving life.

In recalling the passage, he believed that modern policing had ethically regressed, that progress didn't always mean improvement. In his view, the current criminal justice system bore more resemblance to a private circus than a public service; manipulated by ringmasters, its wares peddled by snake oil salesmen, its 'achievements' embroidered, misrepresented, distorted, and utterly failing to produce anything worthy of its lofty origins. The top of today's tree was populated by career men, not policemen. Their aspirations were not in the public interest, but self-interest, a gong and a fat pension followed by a rich career in consultancy and club membership. He knew this proposal interested him but was also aware of the dangers it posed. But if Christian was offering him a real chance to live by his principles, he owed it to the Tom's and Sacha's of this world to make a stand. He also knew that criminals couldn't be beaten by an idea, however noble. It would take deeds. He trod carefully.

"I'll carry out a paper exercise. See what may or may not be done. What will be needed in terms of personnel, infrastructure, our own security etc. Mr. Christian," correcting himself, he remembered the invitation.

"Peter, I've spent most of my adult life upholding the law, I'm not about to go riding roughshod over it in what time I have left. Justice though," Ames paused, aware that his next words might well be a commitment. "I'd like to see some of that delivered."

He sat quietly, rummaging through his scruples, then added, "The Hoods were a special case and Ellen's butchers needed to be stopped. In that instance, it was clear that they never would, unless someone stepped in. It's not a road I'd like to go down a second time. Murder is murder, whichever way you look at it, however we may choose to justify it."

Christian smiled, moved back round to his chair behind the desk, apparently satisfied.

"Set your own salary, whatever you feel is fair. Acquaint yourself with Daniels. The principals you know of, I can never keep up with their names, but I believe they are somewhere in the grounds. And Stuart…please don't feel that you need to report to me. I'm happy for you to do so but consider yourself autonomous. I rarely leave these rooms and your company is welcome at any time. On a corporate note, I have a name for the new enterprise, Themis. I hope you like it."

The 'consultation' ended, and Ames took the stairs down to the lobby, searching for 'Themis' on his phone.

The reference appeared immediately. Themis, one of the twelve Titan children of Gaia and Uranus and second wife of Zeus. She was the goddess and personification of justice, divine order, fairness, law, and custom. There was a persuasive quality to the description. A brief smile flitted across his face.

The ground floor foyer was a sizeable, panelled affair from which a variety of rooms, large and small, some in use, some not, diverged. An open office door immediately adjacent to the main entrance exhibited some signs of life. Ames made for it and entered what was clearly an office. Its sole occupant looked up from the paperwork she was studying.

"Mr. Ames."

He cast a habitually professional eye over the speaker. Guessing mid-thirties, dressed for the office, slim but not skinny; a crown of blonde shoulder length hair, spectacles framing an open expression on a carefully made-up face. Conventionally attractive, her address gave him her full attention.

"Bailey, is it?"

"Yes, Sir. But Daniels is fine."

He was familiar with her voice, having made appointments through her over the phone. It was rich with just the right amount of warmth without implying familiarity. Overall, the impression he got was one of qualified efficiency.

"Peter said I should pop in, say Hi."

She came from behind her desk and offered a hand. "Good to finally meet you, face to face."

"And you." Offered Ames. Judging that the hand he'd just shaken, while manicured, was unexpectedly firm.

Returning to her desk, she opened a drawer and withdrew an A4 buff envelope. "This is for you. Admin and finance."

Opening the envelope, Ames upended it, documents sliding into his open hand.

"There's the usual standard forms you need to complete for me and if you could sign the back of the credit cards, that would be dandy. We're not big on paperwork here, but there are minimum requirements to be fulfilled. I don't want or expect receipts or explanations from you. I will however be monitoring the balance on those cards, purely to ensure the account is replenished as and when required. One is for your personal use, expenses, and the like, the other for work related expenditure."

Ames fished out the plastic and saw his name embossed on each.

"Themis, again?"

"Oh. Yes, due to the nature of our business Mr Christian thought it prudent to form our own bank. It gives us an independence we couldn't hope for under the usual strictures."

"And my credit limit?"

"Basically, there isn't one. And you can withdraw cash, if required. Please forget any frugal habits you may have developed over the years. I honestly think Mr. Christian enjoys seeing it spent. And there is rather a lot of it."

Ames shuffled through the remainder of the envelope's contents. He hated admin, and in order to get it over with as painlessly as possible, sat at a free desk and began to fill it in. While doing so, he allowed his mind to mull over the events of the past hour.

On coming here, he'd expected to return to retirement. The Hood case had been his last, his stomach and conscience unable to take any more. The lump sum and pension were generous, more than ample for his needs and would probably stretch to a home in the sun, something he gave a great deal of consideration to; as a mental exercise if nothing else. He wasn't a golfer but was a divorcee. Changing his status on either didn't bear thinking about. Time weighed heavy on his hands and mind. The contemplation of nothing meaningful to fill his days had ushered him to the Open University where he'd taken up learning Greek, at the back of his mind having

Cyprus as a retirement option. They, at least, drove on the correct side of the road.

A part of his mind grudgingly admitted that fielding for Tom and Sacha had been fun, an added element not usually conspicuous during his police career, and he realised then that he'd missed the challenges of his working life and had really only left the job because of disillusionment. Perhaps he'd give this a go.

He also realised that he didn't mind Christians clear assumption; the cards and paperwork already manufactured, that he'd come on board. Provided that there were to be no more killings, and on the basis that he had nothing more pressing in his life, he was in.

Straightening the completed forms, he passed them to Daniels who nodded, smiling in receipt. He had much to do and was about to leave her office when on her desk, something familiar caught his eye. Laminated, looking something like a credit card but with a photograph, in a smart, leather wallet, embossed with a crest he recognised. Police Warrant Cards.

"Are they what I think they are?"

Daniels nodded and passed them over. Ames studied them with a practiced eye. They looked completely genuine, had it not been for the faces on them.

"These look to be for James and Ollie." He said, noting that the names printed beneath the photos bore no resemblance to their identities as he knew them.

"Correct."

"They look genuine."

"I'm glad you think so. I worked very hard to give that impression."

Ames sighed. *"And so, it begins."* He thought.

"What are they up to?"

"It was their idea. Just keeping their hands in, they said."

There was no attempt at denial, no sense of complicity in what was clearly an illegal act either taking place, or about to. Daniels was either naïve or committed. Reminded of the handshake, he presumed it was the latter.

"What idea?"

She reached into her filing system and retrieved a thin sheaf of documents, handing them to him.

"These were about to go into the shredder."

Ames glanced at the papers in his hand and flicked through them.

"Drugs?"

"Yes, the kind that gets passed around outside our schools. The boys have an office somewhere around here. They study the newspapers and if something catches their eye that falls under our purview, they act on it. In this case it's the dealers that start kids young, hanging around outside school gates. They've come up with a way to deter them."

"Which is?" Ames asked, dreading the answer. His face said so.

"Oh. Nothing scandalous." She said, offhandedly. "They just identify them and show them the errors of their ways."

"How?"

"Again, nothing appalling. They 'lift' them. Fix them to a prominent lamp post with their merchandise still in their pockets; making it easy for the local police to make an arrest and as a final flourish they came up with this."

She produced a small rubber stamp from her desk.

"They apply anti-theft dye to one of these and stamp their forehead. Painless, effective, and difficult to wash off. Even with the help of a smartass lawyer they're out of circulation for days, bailed or not."

Ames studied the engraved design on the stamp. A stylised ladybird.

"They call themselves the Echo Taskforce. These warrant cards give them the ability to wait near schools without arousing suspicion."

Ames turned the stamp over in his hands, curious as to its meaning. Then, he got it. The ladybird glove that had belonged to Ellen Hood and found near her body. 'E' for Echo and Ellen. He had to admit, those boys had style.

He handed the stamp back. "Where are they now?"

"In the bunker, I believe."

"Bunker?"

He knew where she meant but had thought it disused. Out of curiosity, he'd nosed around it briefly on a previous visit, finding little but empty space and signs of abandonment.

Misunderstanding his query, Daniels gave directions. "You'll find it about midway between this building and the gatehouse. On the left, green, steel door set into a mound."

Walleting his new credit cards, Ames nodded briefly in assent and left the building. She went back to work.

En route, Ames couldn't help but acknowledge the subtlety of the boy's operation. He knew from experience the carnage these pushers created. Though kids as young as 8 had been caught at school with cannabis, the majority were in the 14–16-year-old age groups. It was a mammoth problem nationwide that the law struggled to contend with. Any intervention was going to be useful, provided no-one died.

The boys' unique approach to the problem had the added benefit of making the pushers appear ridiculous, their street cred shot to pieces by an indelible ladybird emblem tarnishing their foreheads, the meaning of which wouldn't take long to circulate. It was also clear James and Ollie had not forgotten Ellen. A nice touch.

Approaching the bunker he noticed that unlike his last visit, the worn concrete staircase exhibited signs of recent use, the moss that had once made descent hazardous, now cleared. He recalled that the green steel door that had previously required laborious levering on his part, now opened easily on freshly oiled hinges.

Inside, the atmosphere was as before, still musty, but now mixed with what he knew to be cordite. The report of gunshots led him further, perhaps half a minute on. His route opened into a yawning low-ceilinged space populated by a scattering of old metal chairs and the occasional grey, undeniably 1960's, filing cabinet. An air of disuse permeated. To his left, over in a corner, he could see a more organised area, outfitted with the trappings of an indoor shooting range.

Behind a waist high counter he saw James and Ollie wearing ear defenders and pistols in hand, aiming at targets around 30 metres down range. Shots rang out and Ames held back, knowing better than to startle men with loaded guns. The gunfire ceased abruptly as their magazines were emptied, a grey blue, acrid smoke shrouding the two firers.

Ames watched as the pistols were made safe and laid down on the counter, then, ears ringing, he made his presence known.

"Afternoon boys."

They turned together and acknowledged their visitor by removing their ear defenders.

"Inspector Ames." The man he knew to be James took the few steps necessary and offered a handshake.

"I'm James. This is Ollie." Ames took it, then in turn, shook Ollies hand.

"It's Mister, now. I'm retired…or Stuart if you prefer." He gestured to the range set up. "Keeping your hands in?"

"You never know," said Ollie, with a grin. "And it keeps us off the streets. Fancy a go?"

Ames demurred. "Not just now. Is there somewhere we can chat?"

"Down here, not really." Said James. "But we have our own space up at the house."

With a sweeping motion he added, "Would you like the tour, since you're here?"

Ames nodded, wondering what other changes the boys had made underground. "Why not?" And fell into step beside them. James went on.

"The house you've seen but you might not know it's former use, though you can probably guess." James gestured at their surroundings. "From this."

Ames nodded. "WW11 site, murky purpose, carried over into the Cold War then abandoned and sold off."

"Something like that." Agreed James.

"After the war it was picked up by the Ministry of Defence, just what for we don't know but it was during that period that this bunker was built, perhaps as a political bolthole, communications centre, we're not sure. It's been stripped of everything bar electricity and old bits of furniture. Post-cold war, the entire site was then passed to GCHQ as a training centre. About 10 years ago it was surplus to requirement and essentially abandoned. Until recently, it was earmarked as a housing development until PC stepped in and bought it outright." Ames assumed that PC was Peter Christian.

"We love it." Interjected Ollie. "You actually get your own parking space." Ollie loathed public transport but due to city restrictions, occasionally and very reluctantly had cause to use it.

James frowned. "To continue; Ollie's parking issues aside, it's private, secluded but close to infrastructure and there's masses of open space. We even have an airfield. This bunker is an added bonus. Soundproof and with space to use your imagination."

Ames followed as the two men took him through a diversity of rooms, large and small, each with a purpose and none of it present on his last visit. Hostage rescue, urban clearance and the like, hostile targets peppered with bullet holes, innocents in pristine condition. It was clear that apart from their 'Echo' activities, they'd made use of their time. Ames indicated that for now, he'd seen enough.

Leaving the bunker, they walked together to the main house and to a back room on the ground floor.

It was a base, of sorts. Not unlike any established police operations or incident room. A small kitchen, a couple of desks bearing computers, paperwork, coffee mugs. Ames wandered over to study their latest efforts, a whiteboard displaying intel. Long lens photos of schools and individuals. Appraisals of specific characters. Random inked ladybird stamps which in moments of boredom had been dotted about graffiti like on the pristine white surface. Clearly an overview of Task Force Echo.

With James busy in the kitchen, the sound of cups rattling and a kettle boiling, Ames turned to Ollie who had been studying a computer screen.

"Take me through it." He asked.

Rising, Ollie joined him at the whiteboard.

"We thought we'd make ourselves useful." He began.

"PC took us on permanently after Tom and Sacha were sorted. We didn't have a clue what for 'cos with the twins out of the game his security needs seemed no better or worse than most guys on the street. But we got the feeling he had something in mind, something we could build on for ourselves instead of working the grid. The money is good and prospects bright and it beats running around Angola with a price on our heads".

Ames interrupted. "An occupational hazard?"

Ollie grinned. "More of a bonus." Then continued.

"He said he had someone in mind to head us up but until they were in situ, to crack on with whatever we felt like doing. We had an idea it might be you, and here you are."

Ames let the reference to his position go for now. He was more interested in the boys' motives and thought processes.

"No more killing." Said Ames, pointedly. The Twins may have deserved it, but it still left a stain on his psyche.

"That wasn't us." Ollie replied, matter of factly. "Like you, we were just helping out, but we do reserve the right to act in self-defence."

Ames was unhappy at the thought but couldn't disagree with the doctrine. It took a moment for him to reluctantly agree.

"Fair enough." Then as an afterthought. "Miss Daniels?"

"Ah." Muttered Ollie, suddenly pensive.

"It wouldn't be right for us to tell that story, at least not yet. Maybe later, when we all know more about each other, for the mo, let's just say the three of us have worked together in the past."

Ollie's manner indicated the matter was temporarily closed. *'OpSec.'* Thought Ames. Operational Security which permeated these SF guys bones. OK, he got that and let it lie. He wasn't yet sure himself how deep into this he was going to get but if he was to fully commit, he knew that trust had to be earned. Something that went both ways. He glanced again at the whiteboard.

"You were saying?"

Ollie faced the whiteboard. "Right. So, we know dealers hang around outside schools, supplying, recruiting. We know we can't fix it but damage it…that we can do." He pointed to a photo.

"This is a secondary school near Sheffield, to be honest we could have picked any school, anywhere, they're all afflicted, but this one suited us for lots of reasons, mainly topographical, social. Densely built up, high unemployment, you get the picture. Basically, we sit, observe, and identify. Not difficult. Once we've got the dealers tagged, we follow them and when the opportunity arises, we lift 'em."

Ames raised an eyebrow wondering what was coming next, he was still uncomfortable with what he considered might easily turn into a 'cowboy' outfit. His concerns were eased though.

"Any cash on them we stuff through charity shop letterboxes. Then, in the wee hours, we strap our baddies to a lamppost or a similar immovable object, bag their product up in plain view around their necks, give them the ladybird stamp on the forehead and phone the local nick, using their own phones which we leave behind for the local plod to trawl through."

Ames nodded. "The tip of the iceberg."

"We know," Ollie replied regretfully.

"But it's something, and who knows what kind of gold is in their mobiles." Ollie thought for a moment before continuing. "Anyway, we were bored."

Ames looked away from the intel as James appeared with coffee. Taking it with thanks, he sniffed, hoping the brew he'd savoured upstairs had permeated downwards. It hadn't. Disappointed, he looked over the mug at what he now viewed as his 'operatives'.

Images of retirement and sunny Cyprus receded from his mind. "Well," he paused. "Let's see what we can do about that."

Something Christian had said about Ms. Hutchison had perturbed him and Ames didn't like loose ends. "How d'you fancy a trip to Scotland?"

Hutchisons Last Stand

Taking the M1 and A1, the boys drove north. The briefing from Bailey quite comprehensive, as usual.

Even though a very recent arrival, Ms. Hutchison was already extremely unpopular locally. What was once a vigorous hunting and fishing estate, was now a Zen and Mindfulness centre. She'd apparently toyed with the idea of it being a 'safe place' for migrants, but a few weeks of close contact with 'teenage' men armed with a full and vocal comprehension of their 'rights', and a casual disregard for those of the local womenfolk had seen a retreat from that experiment.

Additionally, her ban on hunting and fishing had caused dire consequences for the local eco system. Relieving the gamekeepers and estate staff of their posts was an immediate and significant blow to the local economy but in the long term, meant no more trees would be planted, no ponds created, no peatland restored, an out-of-control deer population, predator control non-existent, invasive non-native species rampant, as meanwhile, skilled men and women were forced to sit idly by while generations of love, labour, and experience was slowly erased.

The last month or so had seen her making noises to Strasbourg and the European Court of Human Rights. This was her field, and she was determined to get back into it; despite being barred from practising in the UK. She was making inroads too. While she may never regain her former status, the bloody media having turned against her, she felt assured that with a few fresh and innovative successes under her belt in Europe, she might yet be a force to be reckoned with and her unfairly imputed reputation restored.

Her move to Scotland had been 'tactical', the current Scottish government being more sympathetic or supine towards Europe and therefore much more useful than Westminster. She had friends in the EU who were compassionate, and just far enough away to not particularly care of the circumstances surrounding her defenestration. Their habit of being habitually dismissive of the UK would ensure she got a 'fair hearing'.

Slipping from the main road onto a long, imposing driveway, James and Ollie approached the hub of the Zen centre, a grey, granite structure with castle like pretensions; crenelations and flags, the largest of which being the banner of the EU. The reason for this was clear on entering the building, the main clientele being principally European in nature.

To polish their credentials with some diversity, they masqueraded as a 'couple', and Bailey had booked them a long weekend in a double room.

James and Ollie were used to uncomfortable, alien environments but here, they could literally feel their skin crawling as they were welcomed as kindred spirits and offered a whole raft of holistic treatments and mindfulness seminars. That said, their role meant entering wholeheartedly into the spirit of things, disguising the fact that they were scoping the place out.

"I can't take any more of this. It's worse than Karaoke." Ollie muttered.

"I'm with you on that." Agreed James. "We'll do it tonight."

The lab had supplied them with the means. Adey, a shock of black, scientific hair, square jawed, white coated, and their resident technician, explained.

"Right, lads. You've heard of LSD?"

Both nodded.

"Are you interested in the science?" He asked, more in hope than expectation.

"Not really", replied James, "Just the timeline and effects."

Adey's disappointed was evident; as resident 'lab rat', his was a solitary existence and visitors were rare. He went on.

"Effects…It's a hallucinogen, it disrupts how neurotransmitters work in the brain. It's essentially a man-made chemical synthesised from Ergot, a fungus that grows on certain grains, you know, Rye, and the like. It's probably the most powerful one available producing the most spectacular hallucinations, changing the way reality is perceived and is mood altering." He reached into a drawer.

"I made this batch myself." He said proudly, handing them a phial of clear liquid.

"Colourless, odourless, one dose of this and she's away with the fairies, and, though I can't predict what form her behaviour might take, the most likely effect is that she'll appear dazed, unable to speak and become manic."

"How much of that will do the job?" Asked James.

"Well, there's the standard psychoactive dose, say, 80 to 200 micrograms, which is the most common but unlikely to produce the spectacular result you want."

"And the non-standard dose?" Asked James. "C'mon Adey, I can tell from the look on your face that there's a nuclear option."

He sighed. "Colloquially known as the Heroic dose, 200 to 400 micrograms."

"And that will?"

"It'll produce a dramatic change in world view. Invoke death experiences, offer eureka moments, create visual and auditory hallucinations. To that little mix there'll be an additional pinch of mystical experiences. In short, an emotional roller coaster she'll be powerless to withstand."

"We'll take two of those, please."

"Two?"

"We'll need a spare." Said Ollie. "Something to tuck into her handbag, show she's a user."

"Ah." Said Adey, producing a second phial and regretfully measuring a precise dosage. "I was saving this for a rainy day."

They would wait until the effects of the drug had occurred, then 'plant' the second phial.

Hutchison was at the bar, braying, holding court over a group of avid sycophants, consisting principally of an ECHR judge and his numerous staff. James and Ollie reckoned they were the only fee-paying guests in the whole place, clearly, Hutchison was in full lobbying mode. She wanted back in and was fully prepared to pay for it, money was not an object, her recent divorce settlement giving her the means.

Having made sure their phones were 100% charged, and at an opportune moment, James unobtrusively tipped the contents of the phial into her Chablis, or whatever it was, then the two of them made themselves comfortable, sat back, drinks in hand, and waited.

Adey had said symptoms would start anytime between 30 and 90 minutes. It began pretty much on the 30-minute mark. James flicked on his camera, Ollie's on standby, in reserve.

Her expression altered, as if unexpected butterflies were busy on her skin. On the hour, pretty much as predicted, the giggling started, reaching out for objects that weren't there. Then she found one that was, inappropriately touching a particularly well-endowed female intern, arms outstretched, as if squeezing the bulb on a vintage car horn and making a loud honking noise, a huge smile on her face.

The ECHR judge was the first one to bolt, then, as if on cue, the evacuation began proper.

Oblivious to the mini exodus, Hutchison started swaying, as if dancing to music, and began peering, apparently unable to focus. She fell from a chair, then went into full Isadora Duncan mode and began treating the room as a stage, at one point, heaving herself onto the bar, legs akimbo, modesty forgotten.

Ollie whispered. "Did I just see Kenny Everett's ghost?"

"Cupid Stunt." James replied, this was going better than they could have hoped.

Her audience dwindled further. Even the barman found somewhere else to be.

The boys reckoned they had about 90 minutes before the full effect kicked in but if what they'd witnessed so far was anything to go by, this was going to be epic.

They recorded three hours of footage before deciding it was time to go public, cajoling her outside they managed to get her into their car for a short trip to the local village.

They let her out and she was glad to go, the car apparently an alien spaceship and she the abductee.

Nature took its course and the next morning saw her streaking naked down the high street, arms aloft, and screaming like a banshee. The village was small, Presbyterian, and insular.

The sight and sounds of a muddied, crazed, wild haired lunatic doing star jumps in her birthday suit in front of WH Smiths shop window was a spectacle not previously witnessed.

It was 'fortunate' that someone was on hand with a half decent camera, the resulting pictures making their way swiftly to the mainstream media. Ms. Hutchison was headline news again. Camera phone footage, censored on TV, much less so on the internet, went viral, reaching Europe in minutes.

When she'd recovered, her calls to Brussels were no longer being taken and the estate empty of guests.

Ms Hutchison retired from public life.

One Year Later

The dogs were barking yet the sun had barely risen. There was a hint of dew on the lawn that Tom knew the fine day forecast ahead would soon steam off. He turned away from the kitchen window and looked fondly at his wife. Dressed for the outdoors, Sacha was heading for the door when her phone vibrated, alerting her to a text. Picking it up from the table, she nodded.

"The girls are on their way."

It had been a little over a year since they'd handed the Christian twins some rough justice and Tom and Sacha had made good use of the time. They'd remarried. A private affair: abroad, a precaution to avoid media intrusion. Happily, it had either worked, or the press had lost interest in them.

The scandalous, unpleasant, and heavily reported demise of The Twins had briefly renewed Tom and Sacha's acquaintance with the news outlets, but attention had soon switched to 'Mommy' when word got out how she'd messed with evidence; her children's attack on Ellen had been filmed by the twins and had somehow found its way into their possession from evidence, Mrs Christian the only possible source. There had been a further incident somewhere in Scotland. Either way, their lives seemed now to be their own.

James, Ollie, and Sid had attended the wedding, friends now, a bond made through hardship, shared risk, and trust. Sid lived in the grounds of their home in a purpose-built cabin. His official role was handyman/gardener, but all acknowledged that the extra layer of security his presence offered was a bonus.

James and Ollie went off the radar from time to time, but Tom and Sacha knew better than to ask what they were up to. Lately, when occasionally paying a social visit, both boys seemed content and unstressed, which might or might not be a good sign. The boys never alluded to secrets. They were either happy to discuss what they were doing or were inscrutable.

Sid's presence aside, the house had an empty, barren feel to it. Unsaid but understood, they both knew there would be no more children. This left a space that no amount of pointless diversion could fill. They'd tried travelling, socialising, but they knew they were putting too much effort into meaningless and unproductive endeavours that simply didn't fill the void that had been Ellen.

Sacha had always loved animals, even, as a child, once sharing her life with a pony called Peanut. Animal welfare had always been a quiet passion of hers, so, when she enthusiastically proposed creating a shelter…a sanctuary principally for dogs, saying, 'They give more than they take'; but hinting that no fur or fowl would be turned away, Tom understood. An animal refuge was as good a way as any to provide an outlet for her energy and compassion.

In their grounds, close to the main house, a small complex that she had fastidiously designed and overseen had been custom built. The ensuing months had seen a variety of unwanted, unloved, neglected pets brought in for care, treatment, or rehoming. The rehoming part had been difficult at first. Sacha viewing each creature as part of her family but over time it had become easier to let them go, an inevitable flow of more needy individuals forcing Sacha's hand. From the wild, the occasional injured fox, badger, or deer appeared and having been restored to health, were sent back to nature.

Every now and then, an older dog with no chance of adoption made its way into the main house and stayed there. Tom, Sacha, and their own dog Pooh would settle down with them most evenings. Unenthusiastic about it at first, Tom was now a fully paid-up member of her haven project. If Sacha was happy, Tom was happy.

They were in the kitchen, going over the things to do list when Tom noticed a tiny black speck on her top lip. He beckoned with a finger. "C'mere."

They met across the table, and he gently picked the dot from her lip. He flicked it away. "Been in the bins again?"

"It ain't for nothin' you call me an urban fox honey." She smiled in reply, responding to their old, shared joke.

"Feeding time." Said Tom, an ear cocked towards the mounting row outside. It was more of a statement than a question. The noise from the kennels a clear call to action.

"Yep. Then exercise. Don't forget that Inga and Donna will need letting in whilst I'm on breakfast duty...see you in a mo." She rose and made for the back door, Pooh wagging beside her.

"Righto." Tom acknowledged. The barking intensified in anticipation as Sacha went outside and was clocked by the kennels current tenants, Pooh scampering ahead.

Tom refilled the kettle. Sacha's volunteers liked five minutes before getting down to business. Ladies with time on their hands, they were a huge help with the four-legged residents. Donna Woo, her surname of Polish origin and unpronounceable, hence the abbreviation. A diminutive, middle aged, friendly blonde who refused to get too attached to a single dog…then promptly did, and Inga Turner, similar age, and shape but with a shock of wild hair, a vegan and a white witch, quite mad and devoted to animals.

Sacha loved having them around, but Tom hadn't quite got used to the incessant chatter, preferring instead to quietly wander around the grounds with Sid. Tidying, pruning, planting, usually with one of the older dogs ambling beside them. The gate intercom buzzed.

'That will be the girls.'

Tom activated the gate motors, then heard the familiar sounds of a car moving over gravel as it approached the house. Heard it stop, turn off and the sound of car doors closing and footsteps crunching. At the back of his mind something said that these established noises were anything but. Curious without knowing why, he opened the front door. It was James and Ollie.

Themis

"Are you sure about this?" Ames asked, his reluctance evident.

"Yes, Boss." Replied James. "There's no way we can cover all the surveillance needed and what could be more natural than a married couple out and about? Bailey reckons we could even set them up as Social Workers."

They'd started calling him *'Boss'* after a month or so. It sat ok. After Scotland, together they'd accomplished a huge amount in the short time available.

Vehicle maintenance workshops had been built. A forensics lab and an I.T. department created from scratch and housed within the old Jacobean mansion. In essence, everything you might need for the work they intended to do. Between them, Ames, Bailey, and the boys had more than enough trustworthy contacts to fill every conceivable vacancy, scientist, mechanic, I.T. geek, in house security. All known quantities. All reliable.

Taking their cue from Peter Christian, their recent efforts meant that the Themis proposition was now an undertaking.

"There's no other way?"

"Not in the time we have, Boss. We trained Tom and Sacha; we also figure they're motivated. We'd like to at least offer them the chance."

"Just surveillance then? Promise me they won't be at the sharp end."

"Can't do that, Boss." Interjected Ollie. "Goes against the creed. It's not something we expect, and we'll do all we can to see it doesn't happen. But making promises like that…not our style."

They stood in front of his desk, relaxed, hands clasped, at ease in the military sense, waiting for a response.

Six weeks ago, Ames had taken a social call from a former colleague, now a senior officer, Arham Khan. They were friends not least because they shared a conviction that policing should be egalitarian, and reflect societies need for fairness, regardless of social status. Chit chat soon turned to current, frustrating events.

"I'm fucked, Stuart. The higher ups keep telling me that any overt action would be seen as discrimination," Arham was in full, indignant flow.

"Some bollocks about not upsetting community harmony, inciting riots. Twenty-seven point media strategies from fucking morons on worthless committees and focus groups, money spent on gender neutral toilets and tampons in the gents. Fucking rainbow-coloured lanyards and happy paint jobs on police cars seen as more important than allocating resources to boots on the ground, where the fight really is. Headline grabbing 'initiatives' that do my head in. Our so called 'leaders' have taken one diversity lecture too many. The virtue signalling somehow absent when it comes down to actual facts and evidence. They just call these young girls' fantasists and liars. And it's easy to dismiss them, their backgrounds aren't the best, and if that wasn't bad enough my own people; the one's that actually give a shit, think it's me knocking them back. Under instructions from on high, I formed a Task Force, and we were doing great work, but the more shit we dug up, the less they liked the smell of it. It was too big, too sensitive, too political. Specialists are being transferred out against my wishes, one of my best officers has resigned in protest."

Arham had run out of steam but being old enough and ugly enough to understand the old mantra, 'if you can't catch the criminals, criminalise those you can catch,' Ames had caught the drift. There was and always had been an easy way to manipulate conviction rate headlines. He knew full well from bitter experience that some criminal activities were swept under the carpet; it being much easier and cheaper to deal with by simply being ignored and going after the civpop for minor offences.

It had always been a numbers game dictated by politics. But this was bigger than that; this was lies becoming the truth and Arham was talking about the worst of them, child grooming and the gangs that perform it.

"You know me, Stuart. Right?" Ames knew what Arham referred to. His origins were Pakistani Moslem and his progress through the ranks within the police occasionally uncomfortable. Arham was a practising Moslem and prayers at work were occasionally openly ridiculed, sniggered at. Not easy to ignore but Arham did it, having explained to Ames one particularly difficult morning, that tolerance was what Islam was about.

"If anyone could NOT be accused of racial intolerance, it's me. But my hands are tied, and rumours are circulating. Responding to them is not an option. I'm being bent over and fucked from top to bottom." He added wryly, "Something I'm used to." Then continued, "The worst of it is that no-one is doing anything."

Ames had sympathised and when the call had ended, it was Arham's last sentence that lodged in his mind.

He'd called Bailey and the boys in and briefed them on the call. In the ensuing 6 weeks, Daniels had trawled for information and the boys had completed a recce on the affected streets, gathering intel, identifying suspect people and places. What they'd come up with confirmed everything Arham had said, but there was more.

"This is not your stereotypical grooming gang." Ollie reported. "White boys are in on it too. All working together, one great big, happy, multi-cultural family."

It made no difference to Ames other than that it was outside the norm. These gangs were usually tribal. It seems that some ethnic differences can be overcome…if the final result justified it.

"Our problem is that we just can't cover all the ground, all the time. Nor can we just trail the girls involved. They're too young. We'd stand out as creepy. We need a man and wife. A couple. We need Tom and Sacha. Simples."

Back To The Fold

"Come in guys. Come in." Tom was mighty pleased to see them. Aside from the fact they were great company, he got a buzz from recollecting the stuff they'd done as a team. As worthy as an animal refuge was, it wasn't the stuff of Tom's dreams.

"Sacha's on feeding duties. She'll be glad to see you. I'll call her in."

James strolled to the still warm kettle to make a brew. Using the intercom, Tom told Sacha about their visitors.

"She'll be 5 minutes. The girls should be here by then." On cue, the gate buzzed, and Tom pressed it open. A minute or so later, Donna and Inga breezed into the kitchen.

"Morning ladies.... Bacon sandwich Inga?" He asked, with an air of wide-eyed innocence.

"Fuck off, Tom."

Same question every morning, same vegan response. The kitchen was filling up as pleasantries were exchanged. Donna, Inga, and the boys were acquainted from previous visits, so no eyebrows were raised. Sacha bustled in, Pooh inevitably in her wake.

"Well, this is cosy." She remarked cheerfully. After 10 minutes of tea and biscuits, Donna and Inga left to exercise some dogs. The boys arriving unannounced had piqued Sacha's curiosity and she went straight for the jugular.

"Come on then, what's this about?"

Their response startled even Tom, so they took a moment.

"You want us to come and work for you?"

"Yes, Sacha. We need you both."

"For?" she persisted.

There was no short explanation so between them, James and Ollie outlined Themis. Tom and Sacha sat there, unable to do anything but listen.

"So let me get this straight." Tom knew that tone so wisely decided to sit this one out, knowing Sacha was thunderstruck and wanting answers.

"Peter Christian? Ames? Themis? You two?"

Ollie grinned. "Thought you'd like it."

"Like it? Are you nuts?" Her voice had risen. Tom was glad he'd taken a back seat on this conversation.

"For a year? A whole goddamn year, our wedding, social catch ups and you didn't think to mention it?"

"Goes against the creed." Said Ollie, which temporarily ended the conversation and set Sacha frowning.

"Start over." Said Sacha. "I need to take this in."

So, they did. In greater detail. Outlining all that had happened. Christian and Ames's involvement. The logistical build up and personnel recruitment, the ideals, the success of their Echo taskforce, but above all, the motivation.

Sacha stood. "We're going for a walk in the garden. You two stay here. Try to stay out of trouble, please." She looked at Tom and inclined her head towards the door. He knew it wasn't a request and with a wry smile, followed her out.

"Well, that went well." Offered Ollie.

"Shut up Ollie. This is important." James gathered up mugs, cups and plates and headed for the sink. He watched through the window as Tom ambled and Sacha patrolled agitatedly around the garden scattering dew with her wellington boots.

"Jesus!" It was just the one word, but Tom waited, knowing there were more imminent. Sacha was stomping around in a circle.

"A year! Almost a year and they said nada, zilch, nix!"

Tom gave it a moment, trying to analyse what had Sacha so agitated. It couldn't be the request, he knew better than Sacha that the sanctuary, though meaningful, wasn't a cure all for their restlessness. He watched her in silence, waiting for a clue. None was forthcoming.

"Well, nothing to say, Tom Hood?"

He shrugged, a gallic response, his expression bemused.

"Did you know anything about this…this Themis thing?"

"Me? How would I know?" Then he twigged. And smiled broadly.

"Is that it? You're pissed off because they didn't tell us what they were doing?"

She looked across at her husband. It looked like he was enjoying himself. She thought of something to say, her mouth opened but she lost the words. She looked at her feet and shuffled a few stray leaves around, making circles in the damp grass, thinking.

"Yep. Or maybe. Shit, I don't know."

Hearing it said out loud, Sacha realised how ridiculous her attitude was, given the magnitude of what the boys were apparently engaged in.

"Fuckers." She muttered. "They could have said." But she was smiling now.

"Should we go for it? Help out?"

Sacha didn't even take the time it takes to hesitate.

"After what those boys did for us? In a heartbeat. And I love that they're honouring Ellen. Let's go back inside."

James and Ollie looked up as the door opened. Sacha noted how tidy the kitchen was. *"It's the little things."* She thought, smiling inwardly. She liked these boys, no, more than that. She loved them. They were family.

"We're still wrestling with the whole Ames and Christian thing but what the hell. We'll get over it. Me and Mr. Ames are gonna have a little chat when the time is right but apart from that, we're in, what do you need?"

Arranging to meet the next morning at Themis, James and Ollie made their way to their car *'don't forget to bring some clothes...business and scruffs!'* was shouted as they drove away. The gate closed electrically behind them, as if they'd never been. But they had. And Tom and Sacha's world was about to get a whole lot more interesting.

"First things first," said Sacha. "I need to talk to the girls."

Though not really involved in what Sacha was proposing, Tom sat in. Sacha began with an offer.

"How'd you two ladies like a job?"

Donna and Inga looked first at each other, then back to Sacha.

"Tom 'n me need to go away for a while. Family business. It doesn't seem fair to rely on your charity so, I'm offering you both full-time roles…if you want them."

There was a pause while the girls looked at each other, eyebrows questioning. Donna chimed in first.

"I'm up for it. I'm here most of the time anyway,"

Inga nodded in agreement. "Same here, but we'll need another hand. You know how hard it can be with the three of us here, but with you away?"

"Cool." Sacha acknowledged. "Do you know anyone?"

"There's Yvette." Donna smiled, then continued, "She's a teacher but retires in a week or so. I'm sure she'd jump at it. Gotta warn you though, don't think there'll be many dogs left when you get back."

"How so?"

"Ah. Well, she can't help herself. Can't bear to look into a pair of canine eyes and say no."

Tom was feeling like he should contribute. "Anything else we should know? Anything wrong with her?"

"She's half French." Said Inga.

"Jesus." Said Tom. "So, we have an American, a Pole, a white witch and now a Frenchie."

"Half French." Corrected Inga.

"Ok. So, half French. If you're struggling for a name for the shelter, you won't go far wrong with International Rescue."

Sacha smiled. "Not forgetting our resident Australian."

"Not forgetting Sid." Said Tom.

"So, you'll do it?"

Donna and Inga nodded, happily.

"Great. You start today. Ask Sid to find you a little van and set it up with a gate sensor. He's back tonight but I'll call him and bring him up to speed, also I'll leave you with a credit card to cover any incidentals that might crop up while we're away." Sacha turned to Tom. "We should go pack."

Briefing

They recognised the site immediately from when the boys had brought them to the bunker for firearms training, this though, was the first time they'd been to the main house. Daniels had been expecting them and introducing herself, took them through to the Ops Room. The boys were there, as was Ames. He came over, hand outstretched.

"Glad to see you."

"Good to finally see you too." Said Sacha, pointedly, a mild admonishment evident in her tone, with emphasis on the 'finally see you.'

Ames spread his arms apologetically. "If it's any consolation, I had no idea either. I was simply smoothing your way and believed that when that was done, so was I. There was no need for you to know I was busy on your behalf. All this," he gestured at the room, "this is another thing altogether."

Sacha took the apology for what it was. It seemed that when going after the twins, they'd all been part of an orchestra, with the conductor hidden. Given the end result, she held no resentment towards anyone, but was curious to meet Peter Christian.

"Oh, he might pop down. He does from time to time though on this occasion, he'll probably let you settle in first. I don't think he'll ever feel quite right about the twins."

Everyone briefly acknowledged the events surrounding Ellen's death then, to break the mood, Tom strolled over to the whiteboard and the photos displayed on it.

"This is them; I take it."

Ames nodded. "Bailey, if you would?"

The analyst gestured for all to sit then took her place by the board.

"You all have knowledge of elements of this, some more than most. But for the purposes of this briefing, I'm going to assume none of you know anything."

She produced a remote control and flicking it, a screen descended from the ceiling and the lighting levels fell.

"Firstly, Opsec. Operational Security. Usually anything broadcast can be picked up, accidentally or otherwise. Not so with your new phones. They are end-to-end encrypted across all media, spoken or otherwise," She looked over her glasses at the group, as if to ensure she had their full attention, then continued.

"However, anything committed to paper, for whatever reason, demands the use of call signs. I know that you, Tom, and

Sacha, may not be over familiar with this method but believe me, it's mission essential. I understand that you've used Butch and Sundance, previously." Tom and Sacha nodded, mutely.

"You'll keep them. James and Ollie are Tom and Jerry. Stuart is Archer. I am Control. More about the phones later. Are we clear so far?" Silence in the room.

"Some background first. We're fortunate that before our sources operation was closed down, all their intel was committed to a database, which I accessed. This is what we know. Grooming gangs. They prey upon vulnerable, teenage girls, but some are as young as 11. Usually white but not always. They hunt for them, and I mean, hunt, in late-night fast-food outlets, taxi ranks, street corners. That lone youngster trying to fit in but without the social skills or experience to do it naturally. The groomers use cash, drugs, alcohol, flattery, bogus modelling contracts, even the heady promise of romance to create a sense of self-esteem, belonging, adulthood. It's not a state of mind that lasts very long. Not long at all."

Bailey paused then began the horror story proper.

"The first rape is accompanied by a beating or two. Whatever level of distress that induces in their adolescent minds is just the beginning. It's only a matter of time before their 'boyfriend' gets bored or moves on and then they get passed around, while he earns. The handsome, young guy in the flash car they were 'dating' suddenly isn't. From beau, to pimp, in a matter of hours. They go from feeling wanted, valued, treasured even, to being used. Any fat, smelly old man with money or influence can slobber over them and do whatever he likes, whenever he likes." She paused.

"Let's not forget, these girls are still children…yet suffering industrialised rape." Bailey allowed the uncomfortable image to settle in before continuing.

"And they're not expensive so multiple rapes per night become the norm. Queues form. They are just a simple, sexual commodity, traded until they're pregnant, addicts, diseased, or used up. It's rare they get past 16 before one or the other of the former catches up with them, some die, some kill themselves. These are not small numbers. Nationwide there are literally thousands of young girls caught up in this. Stuart?"

Ames stood. "I took a call from a senior serving colleague, the source Bailey mentioned. He is unaware that we are now interested parties. From that call we've identified one particular very busy gang. Forget racial stereotypes, this bunch are a mixture of Pakistani Muslims and scumbag white boy wannabes. Officially, my colleagues' hands are tied. Bailey can explain why." He retook his seat.

"Local councils and police forces, paralysed by the PC brigade and identity politics do nothing. We know they have intelligence regarding widespread and organised child abuse, I've read it, seen it with my own eyes." Her voice lifted in disbelief, as if posing a question, yet staggered by what she was saying.

"But they do diddly squat. Worse, they are occasionally guilty of turning a blind eye. You would imagine that things couldn't get worse? You'd be wrong. If any hints of goings on surface, Councils downplay the scale of the problem, the police are terrified of investigating, even when the girls are threatened with guns or doused in petrol while zippo's are being flicked to intimidate them. They're made to watch as their friends are raped, sodomised, and told they're next if they dare open their mouths. Gang rape becomes part of growing up. All the while the supposedly responsible adults in who's care these children apparently belong are scared shitless of naming names, either because they don't want to be seen as racist; that's career ending in their world, they're spineless, or just plain useless."

She paused, unaccustomed to her emotional response. Her background was military, her usual line of work on cause and effect simple to define and execute, according to laid down principles. None of that applied here, her research into this grooming gang had led her into some dark places. Regaining the little composure she felt she'd lost Daniels cracked on.

"Resources that could be used to police this crime are being side-lined to more PC areas such as extremely well-paid Diversity and

Inclusion roles which achieve nothing on the street. Anyone who is truly diligent is soon side-lined or 'cancelled' for going off message. Anyone who's conscience might get the better of them and report any incidents get clear instructions to walk away, either because of fear or because someone higher up has a vested interest. It's got to the point where it's so commonplace, that whatever protection mechanisms should exist for these girls, simply doesn't. In some cases the police have completely ignored what's in front of them. They actively dismiss these girls as fantasists, desperate for attention, rather than an abused child in need of help. Turned away, these girls have nowhere else to go. I don't know how some of these 'responsible adults' sleep at night. So, evil shysters on one hand, inertia on the other. That, in a nutshell, is what we're dealing with here."

She moved away from the whiteboard, her knuckles white. "We'll take a break, then get down to the bones of it. I'll be back in ten."

Ames followed Daniels from the room leaving Tom, Sacha, and the boys alone. Tom had to know.

"Who the fuck is she?"

Ollie looked at James and said, "She made us pinkie swear."

"I'll just say it was you that blabbed." Replied James.

Ollie shrugged. Having reached some kind of agreement; aware that Tom and Sacha needed to know they were in the hands of a professional, James figured a synopsis wouldn't hurt. Pinkie swear or not.

"She was SRR. Special Reconnaissance Regiment. Her previous address was somewhere near Hereford." Tom had heard of the SRR from rumoured mutterings when he'd served, but Sacha's expression was blank.

James continued. "It's existed since the 70's in various forms under different names. Never numbering more than 150 or so it draws from all branches across the armed forces and as you've seen, from both sexes. There's no need to go into too much detail but here's some pertinent facts. She can drive faster than you, kick ass better than you and shoot straighter than you."

Ollie took up the narrative.

"She can stop a speeding train in its tracks and leap tall buildings in a single bound. Her IQ is genius level. She has a knack for languages and is particularly handy when it comes to forgery...about that...any ID, passport, licence, whatever she gives you, is genuine, as real as it gets. She can get inside systems like a ghost, change stuff, add, and subtract data. You become real. You will exist in that organisations database and have a genuine background. The car you drive will be the real deal and excite no interest other than instructions to leave it be. All you must remember is what she tells you about yourself, which in this instance, is likely to be that you are a pair of earnest social workers."

James finished Bailey's tale.

"Oh, and don't be fooled when she's sitting there behind her desk, all prim and proper, looking for all the world like a librarian." A rising terminal ended the sentence, as if asking a question, then he answered it. "Don't even think about asking what the penalty is for the late return of a library book."

Further conversation was halted as Ames and Daniels returned, half a dozen buff folders in hand. Daniels spoke while passing them around. She'd clearly won an internal battle and was all efficiency.

"In these you'll find what we have on the animals involved. Photos, names, family affiliations, business interests, current occupations. I'd like you to come up with an unpleasant characteristic, unique to each, by which to refer to them over the air. It's just another layer of security."

Bailey opened her file and taking a photograph from it, secured the picture to the whiteboard with a small magnet.

"Number one. Fazawi Alam. Aka, Faz. The apparent ringleader but don't take that as gospel, there may be more influence further up the food chain. It's something we just don't know yet. Mid 40's. Family man, owns several businesses, pays his taxes, is highly respected in the community and a regular attendee at his local mosque. Incidentally the literal meaning of mosque is place of prostration." She looked up over her glasses.

"Not relevant." Then continued.

"As you can see, he is tall, bulky, and imposing and uses all three traits to intimidate. His flunkies have a healthy respect for his temper. He's not a man who likes to be crossed, particularly if a female is the guilty party, worse still if she's white and an adolescent. We know of at least two young girls who have required medical treatment following his attentions. However, you will find no record of this via their NHS records. Faz has an 'in house' guy with extensive medical training. Lately, abortions have been his thing."

Bailey paused, sticking another mugshot on the whiteboard.

"Number Two. Muhammad Butt. Aka, Mo. Another taxpayer and family man, and like Faz, another candidate for Type 1 diabetes. He owns the taxi company that ferries the girls around. Some of his drivers; though not all, perform an additional function, keeping a general eye out for trouble and potential recruits. We believe that in general his drivers know what's going on and often participate, any cost deducted from their wages at source, though their pay packets don't reflect this. I emphasise though that kind of activity is not across the board. It seems a certain level of trust needs to be earned before club membership is granted."

"Next up." Bailey produced another profile.

"Number Three. Eric Johnson. As you can see, white. A building contractor, quite successful by all accounts. His association with Faz goes way back, their business success was built on his overpriced tenders for contracts going generally unchallenged. Pays some taxes, pays more in kickbacks. Divorced, no kids, he's an inbetweeny bopper, was a self-styled stud in his day. Still fancies himself, although that's not an opinion shared by his ladies of choice. The boys tell me his breath is corrosive." She looked over to James and Ollie.

"Brushed by him once." Ollie said, grimacing.

"And last but by no means least," Another photo, this time of a much younger man.

"This little beauty. Badawi Alam. Nephew to Faz. Street name 'Badboy'. As you can see from the pictures, fancies himself as on trend."

The image showed a slim, grinning Asian guy leaning against a car that might once have been a Subaru Impreza; a body kit, after-market styling, and metal flake paintwork turning it into some kind of automotive ten-dollar hooker. Ray-bans tilted up onto his head. Tight, probably expensive clothing, hair slicked hard away from his face culminating in a 'man bun'.

There was a watch on his wrist that looked like it needed a 12v battery. Bangles and finger rings completing the 'man about town' image. The car gave perspective and Badboy was clearly below average height, by some measure.

"He's early twenties but looks much nearer the age of their victims and is the initial point of contact between the girls and the group. He's the charmer that draws them in using the techniques described earlier, the 'boyfriend'. On that basis, he's probably rapist number one." She waited, feeling the dislike build in the room.

"We hear all four offer varying degrees of malevolence and influence but are only the tip of the iceberg. For want of a better analogy, they are the dealers, the head of the snake." Her tone changed, pitching up.

"There are other facets to this you all need to be aware of…firstly, girls go missing. Lost without trace, and very little effort is taken to find them. The easy assumption made is that they're runaways, London bound or some such. Intel suggests that's not the case. It's generally the older girls; 16 plus, the one's that might become more trouble than they're worth, that disappear. It's entirely likely they're being taken out of the country. Trafficked." She paused briefly.

"It gets worse, I promise you. We know of at least one young girl who some years ago became pregnant by one of these individuals.

Her child is now ten years old and female. They are actively pursuing this child by terrorising the mother. Bear in mind that as she was subjected to years of rapes by numerous men, it's impossible to know who the child's father is, so he is very likely still around and involved. One of their number may well end up raping his own daughter." Bailey paused again, allowing that information to sink in before continuing.

"Tasking." She said, putting down her now empty envelope and pointing at James and Ollie.

"Posing as plain clothes policemen, you two are top cover for Tom and Sacha who will be operating as social workers; English social workers." Turning their way, Bailey queried.

"I understand your accent is interchangeable?" Sacha nodded. Clearly their previous engagement with the boys had been discussed.

"Good. An American accent attracts attention, something to be avoided." Daniels paused.

"Your task is to engage with the victims. At least one of them needs to be encouraged to come forward. To us, not to the authorities, they have no trust in the system whatsoever. These girls have been abandoned by society, seeing these dreadful men as some sort of warped security and therefore will be difficult to pry away. It doesn't matter how you do it, but I would suggest some kindness as a starting point. If you can avoid kidnapping, it would be helpful." She next addressed Ames.

"Stuart will be making a social call on his former colleague, Arham. Hopefully he can be encouraged to keep us abreast of any interest in our activities. It's up to you Stuart to establish whether that can be done without compromising our operation."

She waited for Ames to acknowledge, then proceeded onto logistics.

"Cars with the relevant credentials are coming out of the workshop today. Your cover names and history are in your envelopes. You are who you say you are. Be confident in that. I'll make up your IDs in due course". She paused for breath, the briefing almost complete.

"As previously mentioned, you all have new phones. They have a GPS chip fitted so we can track you and you in turn, can track each other. To access the tracking system, cover the camera so your face recognition doesn't work, which will then require you to type in a passcode. These devices differ from all other phones in as much as you have two passcodes. The first is your regular, everyday code that gives you straightforward access to your phones operating system, but the other, altogether different code, takes you straight to the GPS tracker. There you'll find each other. Apart from that, no gadgets, or weapons. A circumstance that won't alter unless or until our targets escalate. You may leave when you are comfortable with your 'legends'."

Daniels addressed Tom and Sacha directly.

"As you two are new to this, I anticipate acclimatising to your identities may take a day or so. In the interim, James and Ollie will take you on a tour of the site and you'll be introduced to significant personnel and their roles. Any questions?"

Sacha was agitated, clearly troubled.

"I have one. But it's more something I need to know." The group waited, while she thought carefully about her next statement.

"It's about our job. You want us to go in and persuade one of the girls to carry on doing precisely what we're here to put an end to. I need to be convinced what we're doing is right. Whoever she is, I need to be able to look her in the eye, send her back in, then be able to look at myself in a mirror afterwards. Tell me there's a reason why we're even thinking of putting one of these girls back in harm's way, I need to hear it. Why are we throwing her back?"

There was a long period of silence, eventually broken, and to Sacha's surprise, it was Tom speaking. His voice was bleak with understanding.

"I think I get it, it's a series of choices, isn't it? All bad but some worse than others".

Turning to Sacha he continued, "Throwing her back, as you put it, is the least godawful option, and while we could just whisk her away, that's not going to help the others…we just have to look at the bigger picture." He added, glumly.

Sacha sat there in silence, processing Tom's words.

James stepped in. "We'll get her out, Sacha. The first chance we get, she'll be out and safe, I promise."

Sacha nodded, silently conceding the point.

To change the thread, Tom posed a question that just might lift Sacha's mood.

"What's the end game? Just handing them to the authorities won't stop any of this." Tom remembered starkly how pathetic the judicial response had been to his daughter's killers.

"We all know what happens. The system, as it stands, is flawed, not fit for purpose. Even if we get these arseholes sent down the custodial sentence will be a joke and it won't be long before they're out, and at it again. What then?"

Tom's angst was painfully evident. Beside him, Sacha appeared equally agitated.

Ollie intervened - Earlier, he and James had spent some time at the site's airfield, testing a theory.

"Me 'n Jimbob have that covered. No-one's going to court, and the punishment will fit the crime." He said simply, adding, "Once we're firm on it, we'll give you the details and if you like, you can refine it, I'm a big fan of democracy."

His accompanying smile implying that not all the participants would be getting a vote.

Knowing the boys as they did, the mysterious response was sufficient. Tom and Sacha had other, less pressing questions but sensed that most of the answers would be in their briefing notes. They'd need to study them carefully before handing them back. Daniels had made it clear that none of the information they held would be leaving the site, and therefore required committing to memory. Her briefing complete, the analyst pulled Sacha to one side.

"You and I need some girl time, follow me." And led her out of the room. Sacha followed in her slipstream down the corridor and into a fully furnished hairdressing salon.

"We need to change your appearance. Any preferences?"

Til now, Sacha had been content to allow Daniels to plough her own furrow, the briefing room being her turf, but as the analyst had said, it was 'girl time'; time for Sacha to do some digging of her own.

"Hold hard, missy. Slow down, girl." Sacha wanted to get this encounter to a different, more personal level. While she didn't figure they'd be going out any time soon choosing curtains together, Sacha was determined to crack open her shell. Daniels intrigued her, plus, she was the only other female in evidence and Sacha enjoyed candid woman to woman stuff, something unlikely to happen between her and Daniels if she couldn't bring down a barrier or two. The SRR operative the boys had described; an adventuress, bore little relation to the aloof, reserved, egghead she now pointedly studied.

"What?"

Sacha thought about the answer to that. Then asked, "Just how long have you been in this man's world?"

Daniels mentally leaned back, frowning.

"I'm sorry?"

Softening, Sacha went on, "You've been around these boys too long, you need to lighten up a little."

Letting that thought penetrate, Sacha sat in the hairdressing station then, plumping her bobbed hair, changed tack. "What do you think?"

She watched in the mirror as Daniels moved quietly into the time-honoured hairdresser's position immediately behind her. She appeared to have regained her poise and her voice had mellowed.

"Well. There're wigs of course. The ones we have here are top quality, human hair. Using the right brushes and conditioners they can be cut and restyled to suit. They have their drawbacks, of course. Some minor discomfort you soon get used to and they're crap if you find yourself having to swim anywhere."

"Ever swum in a wig?" Sacha was teasing, probing.

Side stepping that comment, Daniels continued, "we can add extensions, cut, or radically restyle what you have. If you opt against the wig, a colour change is pretty much essential."

"Carla won't be happy if I'm butchered elsewhere."

"Carla?"

"My regular hairdresser…never mind. Shall we try wigs first and see where we go from there?"

Studying Sacha in the mirror Daniels recommended a darker colour than her current highlighted bob so that it would be more of a match to Sacha's skin tone.

"We'll use wig clips. Once we have them in the right place, I'll sew them in. It'll be secure but easily removable once you know where the fixtures are."

Sacha nodded and sat quietly while several colours and lengths were tried. They both nodded when a good shade and sweep sat shapelessly on her head. Time for some individual styling.

"I'm not the best judge. I've lived a long time with this hair. You choose."

Daniels was cocking her head from side to side, sizing Sacha up.

"Essentially, you have a heart shaped face. We'll start with some free style feathering but keep the top flat. That'll have the effect of balancing your face and softening your jaw line."

"You're shitting me." Sacha had never considered the way her hair was styled to be anything other than complementary to her overall look. The idea that there were techniques out there that achieved more than that hadn't crossed her mind.

"At the same time, we don't want you looking so hot that you stand out in a crowd. So, I'll try to understate what I'm doing. This could take a while."

Sacha relaxed in the chair as Daniels set about the wig. "How'd you get into this?"

"Hairdressing?"

"If you like." It would do as a starting point.

"I've had some training. You see it in the movies all the time. The on the run heroine hacking away one handed at lush locks using only a pen knife, yet somehow, they walk away with gorgeously styled hair. The reality is that changing your image takes instruction, practice, experience and to do it effectively, time. I have hair, I've had to learn to make it work for me, and not just as a cake topping."

Sacha smiled inwardly. Now they were slipping into a proper, 'hairdressers' chat. "You apply yourself to everything the same way?"

Daniels paused before answering, flicking a stray hair from Sacha's shoulders. "You said it yourself, it's a man's world, by working harder and smarter than them, it levels the field a little."

Sacha disturbed the inevitable and uncomfortable lull that followed. Daniels was evidently not big on conversation, at least when it came to herself.

"Give me something to work with here. I figure you probably know enough about Tom 'n me to get us locked away forever. What's your story?"

Daniels thought for a moment; still styling the wig, using the moment to reach a decision.

"I was regular army. Engineers. Word got around that applications could be made to a unit that was 'irregular'. I applied and here I am."

"Honey." Sacha remarked, softly. "There's more to it than that. I don't want state secrets or details, but gimme more than that."

Another pause. Then quietly, matter of factly, Daniels picked up where she left off.

"It was hard. No doubt. Sometimes the way you look can go against you. I was hit on constantly which up to a point, I could live with, but what some of them couldn't get; mostly the ones who didn't get through selection, was that I wanted in more than any of them. And they had nothing to offer me that I hadn't already tasted. I'd have climbed over Jason Momoa to get through that course."

Sacha smiled at the reference. "So, no guys then?"

"Oh, there's been a few, I'm no nun, but nothing too serious."

"Keep going."

To cut a long story short, I was selected for advanced training. Not field stuff…technical, though like everyone, I had a field career. I just got more stimulation from doing the tech. So that was my specialty. Still is."

"The forgery, an' all?"

Sacha saw Daniels smiling in the mirror. "The best part." She said, with a final snip of the scissors.

"Once I'd completed my service, I could have gone to MI5 or 6. I was approached. But when guys like James and Ollie throw something like Themis your way, I couldn't pass it up. They respect me, which is important. Ames has learned to trust me, which I like and as for PC? I think he's just a tiny bit scared of me. I'm in a good place, something money can't buy."

"You could have been a criminal mastermind."

Daniels finished plumping and teasing Sacha's new look.

"I'm not sure you get it, Sacha." It was the first time the analyst had used her given name in conversation so mentally, in Sacha's head, Daniels became Bailey.

"It seems that from here on in, a criminal mastermind is exactly what I am. And I can't tell you just how much fun it is."

"You should tell your face." Sacha said, the joke implied and accepted.

"There's a reason for that." Bailey said, simply.

"Hysterics don't help in this field of work. Professionalism does; but because I'm female, when things go tits up, if someone dies, I'm expected to cry. So, I don't. I just get on with it. Doesn't mean I don't feel it. But there's no way I'm going to show it. There are people that depend on me to get the job done. I'm not about to let them down. I'll make no apologies for that; it is what it is."

She paused, engaging Sacha in the mirror.

"Now for *your* face." She continued. "Let's look at that, shall we?"

Sacha sensed that more probing wouldn't help right now and might be seen as intrusive. A small barrier had come down and an accord reached with Bailey. They were on first name terms. For now, that would do.

"You got a plan?"

"Sort of. The important thing is the eyes. First point of contact and, unless you've done something weird to your lips, usually an individual's most recognisable feature. Your regular regime is something you need to maintain when not working, your normal face will separate you from the one you're about to get. Now, you have round eyes, what to do?"

"Derma fillers?"

"Nope, they can last from 6 to 18 months, and anyway, I'm not qualified. But there's a makeup technique that will open your eyes from side to side rather than top to bottom. A little orange colour can create an optical illusion, if you'll excuse the pun."

Working smoothly, Bailey changed brushes.

"Then with an eyeliner, we just start out thin on the inner corner and make sure the wing is thicker at the edge of the eye, it makes the white of the eye appear just that little bit smaller and voila! You have almond shaped eyes."

Stepping back, Bailey gave Sacha her first sight of the effect. She'd never been a make-up kinda girl and having got over the initial effect, the result was startling.

"Just need to accentuate your cheekbones and select a lip colour and you're done."

Bailey worked for another few minutes then stood back admiring her handiwork and giving Sacha an opportunity to do likewise. She looked different. More on trend and youthful. She felt different. The wig looked completely natural and the face that looked back at her was another character, one about to play a role which in Sacha's judgement, would work fine for the job in hand.

"Ok. We scrub it off and I'll show you how it's done."

Sacha's face tingled. For the last hour or so, multiple applications and removals had given her the technique necessary to replicate the transformation. Bailey was satisfied with the effect and Sacha's efforts so swivelled the chair around.

"Now imagine what we can do by changing what you wear."

Sacha could and got a little buzz of anticipation. This was like going through Momma's drawers as a kid, shuffling around in massively oversized high heels.

"Can't wait to see what you do with Tom."

"Yeah," grinned Bailey ruefully. "That may take a little more time."

Returning to the Ops room was an event. Tom did a double take.

"Oh!" was all he could muster.

Sacha did a twirl, and the boys offered a clearly rehearsed muted round of applause. They'd been here before with Bailey and had an idea the transformation would raise a few eyebrows. A smiling Sacha walked over and stood next to Tom, taking his hand.

"You're up." He followed Bailey from the room. Once the two of them had gone, Sacha looked to James.

"Did I miss anything?"

"Not really." He responded.

"Just catching up was all. Looking good, Sacha."

"Thanks. Just feels a bit weird".

Idle chit chat rolled around the room, waiting for Tom to reappear. Some considerable time later, he did just that. Bailey ushering him in.

Dressed in a dark, business suit, wearing heavy, black rimmed glasses with a blue tint to the lenses and walking in a slightly stooped manner. He had the look of an older man, jaded and heavy with responsibility.

"The overall effect I was going for was when they're seen together, as they inevitably will be, they absolutely do not look like a couple. More a supervisor with a subordinate. Go stand with Sacha please, Tom."

Tom did as requested, and the effect was as Bailey had predicted. The boys ran through their mock applause again and Sacha offered a small curtsey in response. Tom looked ill at ease but that worked too, he seemed a man uncomfortable under scrutiny, a psychological trait Bailey had asked Tom to adopt.

"Right. Let's go and sort your photo IDs. Then you can get out of that gear and relax. It's been a long day."

On Mission

The landscape was depressing, urban and wet. A disheartening, constant drizzle soaking the streets and its inhabitants. They'd driven up 2 days ago in cars prepared and supplied by Neil, one of the new but 'significant personnel' at Themis. Ex 2 Para, a tall, fit cockney with an easy way about him, he oversaw the onsite garage workshop. The cars they drove were outwardly nondescript but 'chipped', transmitting more horsepower than the original manufacturers specs. Comms and jammers were hidden extras. Ollies request for a Bugatti was ignored. *'We're not made of money, mate.'*

On locating the rented house, they unpacked, and set up. There was no need for pretence at keeping office hours. They had no immediate neighbours and sensed that even if they had, no-one would have cared.

The miserable weather that had begun halfway up the motorway and continued unremittingly since, hindered their task. The streets inhabited only by people with purpose. There was no hanging around on street corners, social gatherings taking place indoors instead, any reluctant alfresco participants were generally head down, cursing the weather. They used the lull in regular activity to familiarise themselves with the area by driving through the darkened, mostly empty thoroughfares, tracking down the known haunts of their targets.

An improvement was forecast for the weekend, an opportunity, they hoped.

"Right. It's Friday night. The shit weather is now only mildly shit so there's a chance we'll get a sniff. Take another look at our primaries." Ollie raised a glossy A4 sheet.

"Faz." Then another. "Mo."

Displaying mugshot after mugshot until all four had been accounted for.

"We've seen how they operate and once the girls get into their system, there's no way, short of barging in, that we can get to them until their either going home; usually in one of Mo's taxis, or to and from school. Even then one of their boys can randomly turn up with a sweetener or…a reminder. So, we'll ID the girls, then you two can do your stuff, getting to one of them when they're in school."

"It still doesn't sit right." Sacha said sadly. "That we have to let the damage happen before we can intervene."

Tom laid his hand over Sacha's. He knew how she felt.

"We feel the same." Said James.

"But there's no other way. The damage you speak of, is done. There's nothing we can do about that. And only a girl already involved can help us break this up. The worst part of it is that our best bet is likely to be a girl who's been part of this for a long time."

"If it helps, "said Ollie. "Me 'n Jimbob here figure we can disrupt any newbies being sucked in."

"Won't that spook them?" asked Tom, imagining the kind of disruption the boys had in mind.

"Possibly." Said James, thoughtfully.

"But by the same token, it could take their eye off the ball elsewhere, as in you two. We'll play it as it comes."

Sacha's mood improved a little. The boys going after the recruiters, if not preventing them altogether, would minimise any new victims.

"What sort of disruption did you have in mind." She asked, hopefully.

Ollie answered. "Oh, a little physical chastisement, perhaps some humiliation and some serious fucking up of their pimpmobiles. We're not in a very gentlemanly mood."

"Good. Then let's go find our girl and what school she's at."

The late evening traffic was heavy and erratic. Cars and delivery vans double parked on the high street creating bottlenecks and snarl ups. Horns honking declared impatience, anger, and frustration. Revving engines popping through tweaked exhausts jangled the nerves and simply added to what was apparently the normal chaos.

The usual courtesies were clearly abandoned with the coming of nightfall but that was ok. They'd be lost in the anarchy. As Sacha wound down her window, a conflict of aromas entered the car. Exhaust fumes, spices, the casual aroma of weed.

"Not healthy." She murmured".

"I know that smell." Tom piped up from the driving seat. "I used to grow a bit of that."

"You're not big and you're not clever, Tom Hood. Punch yourself in the face." She replied, a half-smile behind the admonishment. She had to admire the way he'd handled himself last year. It strengthened her faith in his flair for triumphing over adversity.

"Where are the boys?" She asked.

"Two cars ahead." Tom could see their Volvo threading through the traffic.

"Cool."

They hadn't needed to be out tonight. This was an identification mission and that was in the boy's remit. But inaction didn't sit well with Sacha and seeing no harm in it, James and Ollie had agreed to let them ride shotgun. They knew where the boys were headed, so distance between vehicles wasn't a problem. On the other hand, having them in sight was a comfort.

"Nearly there."

They watched as the boys pulled into a streetside minimarket car park. Due to the lateness of the hour, there were numerous spaces available, so they found a spot 20 metres from the parked Volvo and beneath a broken streetlight. Tom switched off the ignition.

They weren't in mufti. There were no plans for them to leave their vehicle and even if they had too, it shouldn't matter. This was a multi-cultural area. Dressed down, in vogue wearing jeans and hoodies, their white faces wouldn't excite attention. They waited with a sense of subdued enthusiasm, knowing that in time, these cocky fuckers would show. Sacha's mobile throbbed. She read the message.

"They're cool. Eyes on. Tonight's about sourcing a girl. If that works out, we get to do our thing."

In the Volvo, two pairs of eyes took in the view. "Nothing's changed." Said Ollie.

The kebab house was brightly lit and busy, glass fronted displays with the usual array of artery busting munchies to choose from. They figured that any new 'meat' was unlikely to show much before ten pm. By then, most of their few options had been explored, pubs out of the question, youth clubs non-existent; and loneliness and boredom gravitated the girls towards the buzz of a fast-food joint. Like moths to a flame. Badboy's car was parked nearby. Unmissable, like a metallic bluebottle, or something from a Batman movie, he had to be around here somewhere.

"Haven't seen her before."

"Agreed." Replied James. Arms folded across the steering wheel. He sat back, retreating into the darkness of the car's interior.

It hadn't taken too long at all. The girl was shivering, her outfit not suited to a night on a street corner, the only nod to the weather, a faux fur jacket which didn't even reach her waist. Beneath a thin print dress her legs were bare and beginning to mottle.

They watched as a young Asian guy, a face they quickly confirmed as Badboy, sidled over, offering her a cigarette. She took it and smoked amateurishly, occasionally coughing while the guy chatted animatedly, smiling, at intervals reaching out and touching her on the shoulder and arms. An invitation looked to be offered and accepted. The boys watched as together; they went into the kebab house. A brotherly greeting met them. All very cosy, reassuring.

"She's being fed and watered."

"Yep." Said Tom. Aware that this wasn't Sacha's favourite part of the operation. It wasn't his, either.

"That's something, I guess."

He turned to face his wife. "Don't stress, she's new. The boys won't let this go too far. Just think of that smarmy arsehole Badboy being taught the error of his ways".

"Ok." Sacha looked towards the Volvo, mentally urging the boys to do something, anything.

Another girl rounded the corner and entered the kebab joint.

"We've seen her before."

"Agreed." Said James.

She joined Badboy and the newbie. An older girl, but not by much, white, who they recalled seeing once or twice on their last trip.

They knew where they were headed, it was part of the pattern. *The pattern*, befriend, reassure; hence the presence of the older girl, go somewhere for a drink.

They knew there was a house nearby that was set up for this purpose. The boys had hope that there was unlikely to be a rape this time around. The third date was the general rule, the second being the introduction to drugs. This was, after all, a long-term investment.

Despite the house being only a short distance away, with a flourish, Badboy produced a remote from his pocket and aimed it at the Badmobile. The older girl seemed bored by the theatrics, but the younger, new girls face lit up with delight as the Subaru responded by beeping and lighting up. Badboy, the consummate gent, opened the front passenger door, offering the prime seat to his new acquisition. The older girl, knowing the game, opened a rear door for herself, and climbed wearily in. Badboy got behind the wheel and fired it up the motor.

"Jesus, fucking Christ, "Muttered Ollie. "Just when you thought it couldn't get any worse."

The object of his disdain had blue tinted headlamps and featured a blue under glow; the whole car appearing to float on air. The interior lit up like a '70's disco and a cherry bomb exhaust popped and crackled, gouts of flame exiting the massive chrome outlet. For a car with a proud rallying history, this one would die of shame.

"Christ, you could see that thing from space. How the fuck is that legal?"

"It probably isn't." Replied James. "But no-one cares."

"The start of the slippery slope. Wasn't it New York that clamped down on the little things, resulting in a drop in major crime? We should use our warrant cards."

James's frown illustrated that that was a bad idea and not one they were going to follow up.

They pulled out from the car park and, even with its rear lights funked up with a dark tinted spray, easily maintained contact with the ersatz Subaru. It was as well Tom and Sacha had opted to come out tonight. It looked like they'd be needed after all.

Agreeing to stay in the car park, Tom and Sacha waited for confirmation of the location of the 'fun house'. Once they had it, they were to go there and follow the older girl home. She was their principal task.

Ollie started again. "And look at that!"

James had been waiting for this. The number plate. Ollie was a classic car nut and registration plates part of motoring heritage and therefore not to be messed with.

"The twat has taken BA88 OYS, closed up the gap, the legal gap mind you, and stuck a fucking screwhead in the first '8'. Do you suppose that's meant to read 'BADBOYS? Now, I don't mind a clever plate, I saw HOT 2 on a Dolomite once and even saw FAB 123 on a shagged out old Mini, but that puts the fuckin' tin hat on it. What use is a warrant card if I can't use it when a real crime is being committed!"

"It's not your warrant card."

James replied, evenly, he was used to Ollies number plate rant.

"You'd best keep up." Ollie replied. "If that thing gets up to 88mph there'll be a burning 11 on the street and we'll never see it again."

"Whatever."

There was now little doubt regarding Badboys objective. They were nearing the house they'd scoped out on last week's recce. Ollie got on the phone to Tom and Sacha.

"It's as we thought. You're up."

Using the onboard Satnav, Tom and Sacha followed directions and drew up near the target house as instructed. They waited for the older girl to emerge.

Lyla

Today was Wednesday. Coffee in hand, they ran over the sequence of events since the previous Friday night.

"So, we know that on the Saturday morning, Badboy took the newbie shopping. Her name is Abby Pearson. She's 14 years old, a baby, barely out of kindergarten. He splashed out on some brand-new clothes for her, a shiny mobile phone, a spot of lunch, and a night on the town. Date number two and sure enough she ended up as before at the house. More drink, very likely some weed, but later when she was taken home, she looked ok. Not tampered with yet, we think. Nothing unusual about that, normal routine, not a care in the world, reinforcing her new status."

Ollie took over the narration. "All very friendly and sweet as you like, Badboy drove her home."

"Any lights on?"

Sacha was keen to establish what the gang's latest acquisition's domestic situation was.

"Nope. A barking dog, probably rabid, 'n the house key under a plant pot. Dead weeds in it though. The garden hasn't been touched in years and the paintwork looks like shit. The place is falling apart."

"So not much parental guidance then?"

"None that we could see."

"Can we get her out of this? Before the third date?"

Sacha and Tom, having been briefed on the grooming process, knew what was coming the newbies way.

"That's up to you." Replied James. "On to the older girl…you guys need to get into her school and do your thing. The quicker you turn her around, assuming you can, the safer all the girls will be."

Tom and Sacha had concentrated on the older girl, who, courtesy of Bailey and the electoral roll, they now knew to be Lyla Dawson. That first night they'd followed her home and, on the Monday, from her house to school.

"We'll do that today."

Practised now, they adopted their 'social worker' identities and drove to the school. Bailey had called ahead, and they were officially expected. They had their fingers crossed that there were no genuine case workers due, but as the school secretary hadn't queried their attendance, 'What, two visits in one day?' were hopeful they'd have free rein.

The school site itself was uninspiring. A bleak and run down product of its environment and lack of ambition or expectation. No playing fields, just a steel railed tarmac zone bordering a tattered 70's two storey eyesore containing what passed as classrooms. There was no investment in the future here, just a failing system going through the motions.

The reception area displayed student art, photos, and achievements. Behind glass sat a frayed middle-aged woman.

Presenting their IDs, they stated their purpose. "Lyla Dawson, please."

"Yes. Been expecting you. What's she done?"

They didn't respond. They knew Data Protection to be an excellent shield to shelter behind.

"Whatever." Muttered the receptionist. "Sign in and I'll make up your passes."

The formalities satisfied, the receptionist buzzed them out of reception and through into the school itself, meeting them on the other side of the door. "Follow me."

They were taken to an ante room. "I'll go fetch her."

Windowless, the room was furnished with a stained, frayed, G plan sofa and chairs, none of which matched, separated by a low, equally antique coffee table. Taking the chairs, they waited.

Presently, the door cracked open, and Lyla entered bit by bit. Fingers appeared first on the edge of the door, followed by a pale, anxious face. Beckoning her in, they stood and offered her the sofa.

This was the first time they'd seen her up close. They knew her domestic situation was less than ideal, but her uniform appeared clean and pressed, if a little worn. She seemed a little underweight which meant that she was either undernourished, on an enforced diet, or worse; on something else. Either way, last year's uniform hadn't needed replacing. Beneath a failed attempt to disguise it with make-up, there were signs of a bruise on her pale jaw.

Bailey had provided them with her school reports, which, whilst not glowing, showed the 15-year-old to be bright and not unwilling to learn, but withdrawn and reclusive, particularly this last year of term. If something interested her, she engaged, if not, she was an indifferent student. She was not expected to shine in education. There would be no career path. She took the sofa. Wary but impassive.

Their roles were different. Sacha had an instinctive empathy, something not in Tom's skillset so he was to stay silent, ostensibly taking notes. Sacha was the lead. She moved forward in her seat; hands clasped in her lap, and directly engaged the young schoolgirl.

"Hi, Lyla."

Lyla's head was down, her face hidden from scrutiny.

"How are you? You ok? "

Nothing. The girl was indifferent, inert.

"How did you get that?" Sacha referenced the bruise to her jaw.

"How d'you think?" Her accent was evident, her voice low, her tone defensive.

"Well, I don't think." Persisted Sacha, softly. "That's why I'm asking."

"Why ask if you don't care?"

"What makes you believe that I don't care?

"No fooker else does."

"Potty mouth." Censured Sacha, needing to set boundaries but said with a degree of tenderness and a soft edge. This girl needed to realise that they held the authority and were willing to use it, but more importantly, that they were on her side. A difficult balancing act. Cautiously, Sacha persevered.

"How did you get that bruise?" She continued, gently. "Who gave it to you?"

"No-one. Cupboard door. I was clumsy is all."

No emotion, not caring if she was believed or not, having played it many times before, Lyla understood the game. She was just verbally filling in the forms until they fucked off and left her alone.

"Lyla, sweetheart. The old cupboard door routine lacks originality. I think you're smarter than that. If you tell me the truth, I promise you we can help."

"Heard that before."

"When? Who?"

"Your lot."

"And if I were to tell you we're different? That we're here to really help? How about that?"

"Don't mean nothing. Never does." The girl still hadn't raised her head. Her monosyllabic replies the only indication she was listening.

"You're wrong, you know." Sacha paused, weighing up her options. "How about if I tell you how you got it. Who you got it from and where?"

Lyla looked up at that. Suddenly fearful, defensive.

"Don't"

"Why? Is it because you're frightened…of them?"

"There's no them." She declared.

"It was me. I banged it on a cupboard."

Now she needed to be believed. Social workers were useless do-gooders who never did anything but talk, talk that got around, and there were people that didn't like it. She fell silent, these two were looking too hard at her. Seeing through her.

"Lyla. Honey. We know there's a 'them'.

Now she was truly frightened. She'd been interviewed before; by bat faced smarmy old cows, or long haired, hemp wearing, friends of Jesus, whose middle class shit for brains hadn't got a clue what she was going through, and if she told them, would run a mile.

"Lyla." Sacha continued, gently, like trying to stalk a wild gazelle.

"Your school reports tell us how smart you are. We know you're pretty much having to take care of yourself at home so that tells us how tough you are. But you can't do it all on your own. You need help. We're here for you."

"Yeah. Right. You're here for me, are you? Do you know where my mum is? I don't. What about when my dad comes home drunk again and there's no food? Or when there's no heating. No way of getting clean? No way out of my shithole of a life? Where are you then?" The outburst was full of hurt and anger, leaving her drained. She slumped, listless and torpid.

"We're not here for that." The man spoke for the first time. "We're here for them."

His voice was firm, determined. That just made it worse. Believing them would just make the fall, when it came, harder to bounce back from. She knew she was at the end of her usefulness to 'them'. The punch to her jaw evidence that they didn't care how she looked anymore. She knew that her looks, and her body was all she had. When they were bored with her, that would be that. She had an idea what 'that' involved. She knew stuff.

"Them?" She scoffed, defiance creeping into her voice. "You 'aint got a clue. You probably even believe what you're saying, but I don't." Then the gloom reasserted itself. "Leave me alone."

Sacha spoke, her words dreadfully accurate. "Faz, Mo, Eric and Badboy. To name just a few."

Lyla's slight frame jolted, abruptly alarmed; as if sensing the sudden presence of a predator. "No! You're wrong! Never heard of them!"

"Lyla." Sacha reached out and laid a soft hand onto the girls trembling arm.

"We know you've been let down. Abandoned, call it what you like. It's why we're here. Because no-one else is."

"You police?" More alarm. This was worse than social services. She'd gone to one of the few remaining Police Stations. A lot of good that did her. They'd really fucked her over, tagging her as garbage and a liar. And word of what she'd done had got around. That had got her a proper beating.

"No. Not police. We know you went to them and got nowhere. We're new, different. We see things through. We want to help you get out. We know how frightened you are."

"You would be. Anyone would be." Her eyes were brimming, cowed, and alarmed.

Tom spoke again. Demonstrating what he hoped was a fatherly, protective tone. "We're not."

The girl acknowledged his presence with a low "Pff!" of disbelief.

"He's telling you the truth Lyla. We're on your side. No-one tells us what to do. If you're ever going to get out of this, you'll need us."

"Like all the rest." Was the sullen response, and her head fell to her chest again.

Sacha moved to the sofa. Sitting beside Lyla, she placed an arm over her shoulders.

"Not like all the rest." The girl cringed at first, then tentatively, but visibly, relaxed into the unaccustomed contact. Her delicate form trembled silently, then shook as she began to sob.

"How? You can't. You won't. You're all fookin' useless! You can't stop it!"

Sacha waited for the crying to subside, waiting for the girl to wear herself out. Then their heads almost touching, spoke softly in her ear.

"We know who most of them are. We know what they do. To you, to other girls. We know about Abby. What they made you do. We can stop it. All of it."

Lyla looked up at Sacha. Guilty, defensive. How the fuck did they know about Abby? Nothing had happened yet. "They make me do that. It's not my fault."

"And that's how you got the bruise, Lyla. You tried to say, no."

"I did. I did try. It's not my fault. I tried."

"They're going to make you do it again…if they're not stopped. You know that."

Almost in a murmur, as if ashamed, Lyla continued. "That's not all they do. They make me do other things. Disgustin' things."

"We know." Said Sacha. "And it's going to stop. We just need a little bit of help. From you."

Lyla lifted her tear-stained face, eyes red from crying, the bruise more evident now most of the make-up had been washed off. And she was tired. Tired of being what she was, what she knew she'd become. She looked at these calm, confident people and bit by bit she wanted to believe.

She surrendered. "What help?"

"Can I see your phone?" Asked Sacha.

Street Cleaning

The weekend was looming and with it, the threat to Abby. Lyla had tearfully agreed to carry on as 'normal', her phone now modified as a permanent recording device. When the tears had stopped flowing, they'd seen signs of determination surface. She made them repeat their promise, then said, 'I'll do it.'

No-one was happy about leaving the girl in situ, but it was the only choice if they wanted to chop the head from this particular beast.

"We might be able to disrupt proceedings. Stop or at least delay Abby's pick up." Ollie had more than one motive for the suggestion.

"How so?" Queried Tom.

"I've taken quite a dislike to Badboy. That oily fucker is a bottom feeder but take him out, and the chain is broken. I'd like to have a chat, or fuck up his transport, he loves that Japanese Cadillac piece of shit. Both options have a certain appeal to me."

"Then why not do both?" Said Tom.

"Guys." James: the voice of reason.

"We can't go off half-cocked. I know what a bitch of a situation we're in, but it is what it is. None of us wants to see these girls being put to the sword but moving too quickly now…well we don't know how that will blow up in our faces. We're relying on your girl Lyla seeing this through. Not ideal. She's been in there far too long for us to be able to predict what she'll do if things go pear shaped, but we need to hear what goes on in that house, not the abuse, no-one wants to hear that, and if it starts, we'll figure something out, but we need to have ears on the cosy little man to man chats. We need to know if what we're seeing now, is the sum of it, or if there's another dimension. Some kind of official involvement, the higher ups."

James paused, thinking.

"But I do like the idea of creating some friction in that house. Fucking up the status quo might get them agitated and in conference as a result. I don't like the idea of direct confrontation, your 'chat', Ollie, but we could fuck up their transport, it might derail at least some of the less savoury goings on, but it needs to look like mindless vandalism, random shit that just happens."

"Leave it with me." Badboy had fucked up what was once a nice motor. Ollie intended to finish the job.

"Sorry, Ollie. Not going to happen. Random or not, whatever we do still needs planning and professionalism, no one is wandering off solo. That said, what did you have in mind?"

"Fair enough." Ollie replied, James's logic overcoming his desire to cause some mayhem.

"I'm now officially downgrading my original total annihilation concept to one of cunning and subtlety." He grinned happily at the thought of action, however small.

"Disable his key remote with this, courtesy of Neil." Ollie held up a small, black fob.

"Superglue in the locks and a knife through all four tyres. Badboy might be able to get one problem solved tout suite, but those locks will take some sorting. Plus, it won't write the car off; therefore, hitting him in the pocket, insured or not."

"We'll do it tonight. What about the taxis? They'll just send one of them instead."

That stirred a memory for Tom, remembering back to the war that, according to politicians, wasn't a war, unless of course, you got caught up in it on one side or the other.

Thirty years of conflict, over 4,600 dead across the spectrum. Countless numbers maimed or scarred for life. Northern Ireland, the so called 'Troubles'. One aspect of which was the hijacking of buses which were then torched and used as barricades. With the buses burned, public transport had ground to a halt. Then some bright spark suggested Black Cabs be brought over from England and large numbers of these were controlled by the IRA. This worked ok until a loyalist gang, 'The Shankhill Butchers', took advantage of this misplaced sense of security and used black cabs to lure and kidnap Catholics at random, eventually casually murdering 23 people.

The groomers had, perhaps unwittingly, adopted the identical tactic but they were using Mo's firm, not black cabs as they were too regulated. Private hire cars that, while outwardly legit, ferried the girls around and kept an eye on the streets. They could turn this around but with a much less deadly intent than the Shankhill mob, and easily supplant Badboy's trashed pimpmobile.

"Clone a cab." He said simply. Then explained his thinking.

"Brilliant. Should have thought of that before. Nice one Tom." James got on the phone to Neil. Requirements were stated and within the hour, Neil called back.

"It'll be with you in the morning, for extra wheels I've asked Dave to bring up a closed panel van at the same time...you never know."

"Ok. Ok." Sacha interceded. Abby's third date was now not a foregone conclusion and for the time being, could be set aside, but as important as that was, it was only a distraction. She had Lyla on her mind, the promises she had made troubling her. Time for some focus.

"So, Trash Badboy's car. His pride and pocket will be dented, his reaction could cause some minor chaos, hopefully a conflab, and it temporarily stops Abby's pick up. Neil takes Abby on a magical mystery tour. What about Lyla?"

From Tom. "Run over where we are again?"

Sacha stood up for emphasis.

"She's scared. More so now she believes there might be a way out, so there's the worry she could fall apart. Christ, she's only a kid. Her mobile is essentially now a bug. Now that we figure we can get Abby out of the frame, we can bring Lyla's extraction forward. I'll get in touch and ask her to go on as normal, then, as planned, she drops her phone somewhere inconspicuous so we can listen in. Originally, I thought we might have to leave her there but taking Abby out of the picture changes that, we can't leave Lyla with her ass hanging out to pick up the tab. She drops the phone, feels sick, gets out and we pick her up. It's over for her."

"Sounds like a plan." Said Ollie.

James agreed. "Right. We chill tonight, wait for Neil's taxi, then waste Badboy's car."

"I'm just popping out for some superglue." Said Ollie, cheerily.

"Bastards!" Fuckin' dirty fuckin' bastards!"

His car was wrecked. All four Goodyear Eagles knifed, flat, and useless. His remote was a worthless piece of shit that no amount of thumbing and swearing would fix, when he'd tried to open the doors with the key, the locks were jammed solid with crap.

Badawi Alam; Badboy, stood impotently next to his prized Subaru. He didn't know why someone had fucked with his wheels but whoever it was; and he'd find them, they were in for some deep, painful shit. Meanwhile, there was that dumb, white slut to be picked up. Tonight, was her big night and he'd been anticipating it all day. He'd tried to get her to send him some pics, to whet his appetite and reinforce control, but so far, she'd resisted. Just some crappy underwear shots, it's why he'd bought the flimsy garments. *Let me see you in them, baby. Wow! Fantastic! You should be in Vogue, baby. What you got underneath for me?'* But she'd refused, *'someone else might see'.* That was gonna change big time, and soon.

"Fuck man! Send a cab. I'll tell her it's coming."

Abby saw the car through her bedroom window. She'd dressed carefully for tonight. She wore Badboy's favourite outfit, the one he'd bought for her, all of it. He especially wanted her to wear her new pants and bra, the set she'd sent the photos of. It was the start of adulthood; she knew someone was going to have her so it might as well be Badboy. He was nice, kind, said how pretty she was, bought her stuff. She really liked her iPhone. *'It's got a great camera.'* He'd said, with a wink. She loved his deep, brown eyes. She might let him go a bit further, she thought. He'd told her she should be a model, that he knew a guy and that he wanted to meet her tonight to talk it over. She'd bathed carefully. Her Mum would be mad, she'd used the last of the hot water. They were always banging on about how much she cost them, how painful giving birth to her had been, how they slogged to put food on the table and how pointless all their hard work was because she would never amount to anything. Well, she'd show them, when she was a famous model.

Neil saw her exit the house and totter down to where he waited, the cab sign bright on his roof. She clambered in and he acknowledged her with a brief raise of his hand; cockneys being in short supply in this part of the world. He put the car into gear and drove her away, as far away as he could get her, his signal jammer silently active.

"She's not there."

His Scooby fucked over, Badboy had been forced to walk to the 'fun house' and he was in a malevolent, brooding mood. "Waddya mean not there? I told her to wait for your cab."

"I'm just telling you man. There's no-one home."

Exasperated, Badboy opened an app on his phone. All the girls were treated to a new mobile as early in the relationship as possible. The purchase had a twofold purpose. Firstly, it was part of the initiation, the giving of gifts essential to their sense of place and new importance. But secondly, and to Badboy's mind, more importantly, the app he installed before handing it over meant he knew where they all were, all of the time. Find My Phone tracked them down to within a metre. He studied the map; and straight away could see Lyla's indicator. She was with him, Faz, Mo, and Eric in the room and it was immediately laid over his own, but no capital A for Abby. The dumb bitch must have let her battery die. Nevertheless, Badboy flicked through his contacts and called her number. No answer. Tonight, was going from bad to worse. First his car, now this.

'Dumb bitch!' As pointless as he reckoned the exercise would be, it was time to place the responsibility elsewhere. "You! Lyla! Get her on the phone!"

Lyla was trembling, terrified. She knew all she had to do was dump her phone and get out. But now she was the centre of attention. She tried to call Abby, deeply suspecting there'd be no answer. That meant she'd be in the frame, she was stuck; vile memories and fear coming to the fore. She hated this house. She hated it and all it had done to her. She hated these men. The fat one, Faizan, or Faz. He liked to slap and bite while he fucked her. He'd punched her last week, a 'love tap', he'd said. He called her names and liked to watch while his friends queued for her. She had to get out.

"She's not answering." She offered, timidly, trying very hard to hide any sense that she might know why.

Faz was not happy. He liked his Friday nights, particularly when the new ones were broken in. He knew he'd be second or third in the queue, but that was ok. Better even. By then, the crying had usually stopped, whimpering had an annoying way of putting him off his stroke.

Badboy busted them first, it smoothed the procedure. The whole 'boyfriend' thing making it seem like a natural progression, drink and drugs loosening their grip on their knickers. Some of the dumb tarts even anticipated it, enjoyed it, at least until the bedroom door opened and a strange face walked in, unbuckling his belt. But if the handover was difficult, if the screaming persisted, Faz went next.

His presence, authority and the random slaps subdued any pretence that this was romance. Their expressions were his second favourite thing. He'd seen them the first night, after the initial pick up. Wide eyed and important, looking and feeling taller. Their new status worn like a badge of honour. He was Faz. The Daddy. But when the pretence was over, when the fun started, he loved watching that veil drop; he felt a deep satisfaction in his gut when the little white bitches got spread for him. They thought they understood what was coming. *'Truly'*, he thought. *'Ignorance is bliss.'*

The first time they got it up the ass was, for him, the ultimate pleasure. They had to be gagged and held down for that. For some time now though, boys had been on his mind. He'd have to dress it up as customer demand. He stroked himself through his clothing.

'Soon.' He thought. *'Very soon.'*

Badboy was bleating on about his car, his mind not on the important stuff. The other guys, Eric, and Mo, were lounging, drinking, smoking weed, talking shit while he was expected to deliver. If this didn't get sorted out, and soon, he'd have some uncomfortable explaining to do to the man upstairs. He glanced over to the only girl in the room.

Lyla, or whatever her name was, wasn't even close to what he'd expected tonight but if it came to it, she'd have to do. He was just too idle to wank. "You've got an hour to find her, or you're 'avin' it." He waved an arm around the room full of men, his words full of meaning that he knew she understood. "All of it! You got me, little white slut? Or do you want another 'love tap'." He raised a clenched fist for emphasis.

Lyla nodded mutely, close to tears. She had to get rid of her phone, get out of this place. Part of her recognised that if that woman from the social was feeding her bollocks, she'd had it; any optimism she'd felt from just one lousy visit dissipating swiftly under Faz's threat. This was the world she was living in, where Faz ruled, one of terror, not trust. That snooty cow was probably at home with her feet up. She wavered, her hand on her phone, wanting to let it go, leave it in her pocket, then, remembering the certainty that she was near the end of her usefulness here, knew she had no choice.

Other girls had disappeared. She'd heard Faz, his coarse laughter, the word 'traffic', scattered here and there. She wasn't as dumb as they thought. Emboldened, she took her coat from the arm of the stained sofa and shielding her actions with her body, slid the phone between the cushions. *'That's me done.'* She thought, relieved. *'I'm gone.'*

She felt the back of her neck tingling as she left the room, almost certain that her actions had been witnessed and that the questions and beatings would come next. She felt her legs trembling but willed them, and her, from the house. Feeling strangely naked without her mobile, Lyla walked with an eye constantly over her shoulder. Any number of unpleasant scenarios presented themselves in a fever of fright. At any minute, Badboy might appear, a driver could pull up beside her, her name called out in the dark. Her head a ball of fear and confusion, she knew she'd have no excuses to offer, would probably blurt out the truth and that would be the end.

That walk felt like the longest ten minutes of her life and her face twitched with relief when she saw the waiting car. She clambered quickly into the back seat. Not quite panicked, but close. "Get me away! Get me away!"

"Are you getting this?"

"Loud and clear."

Lyla had come through. They'd heard the threats of violence and abuse from Faz, that Lyla would be taking the place of Abby; someone that the frightened girl knew wasn't coming and they were relieved she'd got out having done as asked. Once the girl had hidden the phone and left the room, the conversation had gotten interesting.

"Forget your fuckin' car, boy." Faz was talking.

"If we 'aint got that new bitch we got nuffin. I got booze, coke, and Mayfield parked upstairs. He aint gonna wait for ever. Now you either get out and find her or find another one. Pull one off the street if you have to!"

"Fuck that, bruv! They need preppin'. I can't go draggin' girls off the street. There's CCTV everywhere and a straight-out snatch'll see me fucked!"

"Rules have changed Badboy. Those are your options. Sort it!"

"But the cameras?!"

"Don't worry about it. The footage will get lost. You need to do the same. Now!"

Takedown

James looked up from his notes. "That changes everything. Ollie, get on to Dave, looks like we'll need the van after all and sharpish, we know for a fact Badboy 'aint gonna find Abby, and we can't allow a random kidnapping."

Over the mic, he briefed Tom and Sacha. "We have to move the schedule up and start street cleaning. It's not ideal, but we are where we are."

Sacha spoke in his ear. "Two things before we go. First, who is Mayfield, and second, how do you suppose they 'lose' camera footage?"

"My guess," said Tom, joining the conversation, "Is that the answer to the first question may explain the second. Faz sounded worried about upsetting this Mayfield guy. He might just be who we're looking for. The top of the tree. I'll call Bailey. See what she can dig up."

"I'll go and deal with the low hanging fruit." Said Ollie, grabbing his jacket. "Can't have Badboy running loose."

"Wait up." Said James. "Coming with you."

Badboy was stressed. He needed to go and 'skin up'. Taking a side street, he was looking for a dark place to think. Used to being in control of what, until now, had been a smooth-running operation with 'benefits', losing the skinny white slut was nothing compared to the kidnap order. That was a new one and if it went wrong could result in him doing time; something him being so pretty didn't bear thinking about, on top of that his 'Scooby' was fucked. The memory angered him and inspired a desire for revenge upon someone, anyone.

He checked his app, looking for Lyla. Confused, he saw that she was still at the house, yet he knew she'd left. He'd call, see what the fuck was going on. With his head down and his concentration elsewhere he suddenly found his pathway barred by some old white geezer, face averted, apparently concentrating hard on the pavement. Dropping his shoulder, he went to go straight through, no apology intended. He was Badboy, these were his streets, and everyone knew it. If this old twat needed a reminder, Badboy was just the man to give it.

Any preconceptions Badboy had about the next 5 seconds were abruptly and violently dispelled. As Badboy had dropped his shoulder for the anticipated encounter, the old guy had stepped to one side, spun behind him, and powered a rock-hard palm between his shoulder blades. The force of it emptied his lungs in a whoosh of expelled air and Badboy's forward leaning intent was transformed into an uncontrolled headfirst momentum which ended in a painful, bloody collision with a lamppost. He staggered and fell to his knees; more pain, then felt his collar grabbed from behind.

"Sorry, mate. Let me help you up."

With deep satisfaction born of dislike, Ollie grabbed the conceited man bun and pulling hard, yanked Badboy to the vertical, forcing tears from the now upright, but sagging Badboy's eyes. He was slammed against an unyielding brick wall, another shock to the senses, another layer of pain.

Some breath came back. "What the Fu…!

A whisper, close to his ear.

"Shush now, Badboy. How's your car?"

Ollie reflected on the poor Badmobile, how it had been transformed from a design classic to a complete tart.

"What were you thinking, dickhead?"

Confusion was replaced by realisation. Whoever this guy was, he was no old man but a hard bastard, and Badboy knew he was no match for him.

Thoughts of kidnap, Faz and Uncle Mo were replaced by how to survive. He put a hand to his face, smarting, grazed by the lamppost. His attacker stepped back, relaxed, hands in his pockets. What Badboy had taken for a woolly hat, he now saw was a full-face balaclava. Still trying to take this in, Badboy sensed another presence nearby but didn't dare take his eyes from Mr Evil. Not as old as he'd thought. Grimmer than the old white geezer he'd thought him to be.

"Waddya want! You're making a big mistake!"

The presence he'd felt earlier materialised in the form of a second, similarly clad man. He spoke.

"I hope your affairs are in order. You're going for a ride."

Fuck! Now there were two of them.' Badboy cringed, eyes darting, on his toes, looking for a way out. A quiet, black panel van had cruised gently alongside. A side door slid open on greased runners. A dark bulk emerged.

"Bag him." Said James.

Badboy tried to run but hadn't made a yard before being brought down. "True to form." Said Ollie.

"Oh, yeah." Said the big man, slipping a dark sack over Badboy's head.

Dave the Tackle was less of a name, more of a well-earned reputation. Former SBS, Dave was multi-talented. His gig was procurements, there wasn't much military hardware Dave couldn't quietly find and obtain but he also had a flair for clearing and blocking paths, human and logistic, tonight though, he was Neil's wing man, a second driver.

Hands secured with plasticuffs, Badboy was bundled into the van, strapped to the floor, and, feeling the cold steel of a hypodermic enter his arm, driven quietly from the streets he'd thought he owned.

"I've always liked Dave." Ollie mused. "I played rugby against him once…never again."

James nodded. Watching as the van disappeared. "One down, three to go."

A moment later, the only trace of Badboy was a smear of blood on a lamppost, and some torn out hair. The promised rain would take care of that if anyone cared to look.

"I've got an update from Bailey." Tom spoke into his phone, the loudspeaker on.

"Peter Mayfield is Deputy Mayor and PCC. Police Crime Commissioner."

"That's interesting." Replied James, miles away, on the other side of town, watching the 'fun house'.

Tom and Sacha realised Lyla knew Mayfield when they heard "Fat cunt" coming from the back seat of their car.

Sacha turned around.

"You know this guy?"

"'Course I do. You wanna know how he likes to do it?" She answered, through a clenched jaw.

Sacha saw the change in attitude, in bearing, Lyla's earlier panic and distress was morphing into fury. There would need to be an outlet for that. The loudspeaker interrupted her thought process.

"Explains a lot." They heard Ollie say. His voice amplified, tinny.

"Complicates things too." Interrupted James. His mind on the bigger picture. "PCCs can't just disappear. Too much heat. We'll have to finesse our approach. It's time to bring Ames up to speed."

"Done." Said Tom. "He's been working alongside Bailey. What we know, he knows. He's having a chat with his mate, Arham, as we speak."

"Well, they both need to hang fire," said James, suddenly wary of interference.

"We've got a busy couple of hours tagging and bagging. The last thing we want is plod. What's Neil up to?"

"At the seaside."

"What?!"

"He was in touch not so long back." Sacha explained.

"Said he and Abby we're getting along just fine. Without going into too much detail, he's filled her in on what was planned for her. That he's not kidnapping her, he's protecting her. Took a little bit of persuading but eventually she got it, even asked if she could keep the phone and clothes. She's just a kid and not thinking too far ahead. Last I heard, they were eating fish 'n chips."

"I get it." Said James. "But that leaves us a man down given the new situation."

"I'll call Dave." They heard Ollie say.

In the van, Dave was enjoying the stillness, nothing other than a soft snoring from the rear. Then his phone buzzed.

"We're going to need you over here, Oh, and the back of your van is going to get very crowded."

Knowing where 'over here' was, Dave, careful not to excite attention, swung the vehicle around and accelerated towards the action.

"Where is she?" Mayfield had been reasonably content. He had booze, he had coke, but now he was short on time, and patience. This was not a good place for him in which to be seen; he preferred to keep his distance from Faz and his operation. But the tug was always too strong, the need overcoming his caution. There was also the issue of the 'favours' he did Faz. Greasing the wheels, maintaining the status quo. What had begun for him as purely a financial transaction, had morphed into an unacceptable risk. He felt he'd covered all the bases using all the old tropes. The need to eradicate racism and white privilege within the police. Social services rendered hopeless through political correctness and bias training. Complaints disregarded by manipulation of the weak and ineffectual justice system. The social status of the girls making it all too easy to ignore any cries for help. And it was the girls that he was here for.

"Well?"

"I'm working on it, Pete."

Mayfield disliked the familiarity of the address. He was 'Sir', in every sphere bar one, and he expected that omission to be rectified in the honours list very soon. Maybe then he'd spend his time somewhere in South-East Asia. Off the grid but in touch with the things that made life feel just that little bit better.

"Well, get a move on. I don't have all night."

Faz left, bitter and unhappy. Badboy had gone silent, and that kafir bitch Lyla hadn't come back yet. Not that she was any good for Mayfield. He liked them fresh and frightened and Faz thought he had seen something in Lyla's eyes tonight. A look he didn't like. Perhaps it was time he moved her on.

He thought briefly of dragging a couple of girls from the cellar, but they were due to leave soon, also, they were a mess and only good for what they would bring on the market.

Faz had a sense he was losing control, that the system was unravelling. Perhaps it was time to crack a few skulls, slim down the system by cutting out some dead wood. If he couldn't produce, if Mayfield left, displeased and unsatisfied, Faz's leverage was diminished. *'Where the fuck was Badboy?'*

In the van, they all knew that the first rule of battle is that no plan survives the first contact. It was a chaos the three of them were well used to and planning on the fly was second nature. They were perhaps a hundred meters from the 'fun house', parked on a darkened side street.

"We need to separate them somehow."

With an upraised palm, James forestalled what he figured Ollie was about to say, cutting him off. "Yes, Ollie, I know we could probably handle them all but 'probably' doesn't cut it. So, any ideas?"

"Him?"

Dave jerked a meaty thumb towards the back of the van where Badboy lay, a crumpled shambles, he was the link.

Picking up on Dave's train of thought, Ollie rifled through Badboys' pockets looking for the pimp's phone.

"We could text? They've got to be wondering where he's at?"

It made sense. "OK. Read through then figure out how to make the context and style right. What do we send?"

"Let's give Faz what he asked for."

They huddled over Badboy's phone. Scrolling texts, identifying key words. "Send it."

Faz's phone throbbed in his pocket. "Thank fuck for that." Then, "Shit!"

The message from Badboy read. "Got Two. Sweet. Fresh, but need a bro' to run block." There was a location added.

So Badboy had come through. Two was a bonus but he needed help bringing them in. Faz knew his face wouldn't fit, but at a pinch, Eric looked ok, he was dressed right and if enough cash were flashed, he'd be honey to the bee.

Faz sent Eric out to meet up with Badboy, only the promise of new girls stifling any thought of this change in the hierarchy. Eric didn't do street stuff. He paid his money, did the favours, and took the candy. He didn't see it as rape, by the time the girls got to him, they were compliant. The back of his mind registered that some of them might be a bit young, but familiarity with the process took the edge off that.

"It's Johnson." Ollie said. "Easy."

They figured Johnson to be the weakest link. Not tied to the group by family or religion, his only motivation was the sex. His money allowed him to buy some style, mid-thirties, ginger hair, florid of face, he needed all the edge he could get. His star was fading with the ladies. A one-time stud with pulling power; too much good food, bad drugs and booze had dissipated whatever genetic blessings nature had bestowed.

Head down, Johnson cursed having to leave the house. There was a cold breeze that whistled uncomfortably around his midriff. The bottom of his polo neck jumper and waistline of his trousers not quite meeting. He tugged his trousers up, the belt ineffective against the ride under his paunch. He was thinking of his teeth. He was going to need veneers soon. He cupped his hands around his mouth, breathed out, and sniffed.

He never saw them coming. A blow to the back of his head sent his brain into a violent confusion, he went limp, his arms useless by his side and his legs gave way. Falling to his knees, he barely felt his skin scrape against the unyielding pavement. The back of his collar was grabbed and yanked upward just before he face planted.

Offering no resistance, his was a blinking, owlish outrage as his world went from bad breath to bad karma. In seconds he was sacked, hogtied, and bundled into the van. His domain was dark, malodorous, and terrifying. He heard voices.

"Two down."

"That just leaves Faz, and Mo."

"And our friendly, neighbourhood PCC."

"Divide and conquer?"

"Madness not to. Give it five, then send another text."

Eric shut his eyes and tried not to think about what was coming. He flinched as he felt a hand on his arm. Someone chuckled. "You're just going to feel a little prick." Then the sting of a needle. He didn't feel oblivion, just dropped quietly into it.

"For fuck's sake!"

Faz's phone was the cause of the irritation. Another text from that fuckin' useless Badboy. *'We need a car.'* It read.

Mayfield was getting on his tits, the more coke and booze he got inside him, the more belligerent and demanding he got. Faz was juggling morons. He felt a cold ball of fury building and knew of only one way to relieve it. *'Where's that skinny bitch?'* Lyla was still

AWOL. Beginning to sweat, the decision-making process disturbing what should have been a regular Friday night, Faz figured it was time Mo lent a hand.

"Oy!" He lashed out with a bare foot. "Go and get those fuckin' idiots. I'm losing patience."

"Can't drive. Send a taxi." Muttered Mo, heavily under the influence. That thought caused a back problem to resurface. *'Where the fuck are the taxis'* A wiser, less troubled man might have given this question more consideration. But Faz wasn't in a considerate mood. He took another look at Mo, then got really uptight, knowing he'd have to go out. *'If you want a job doing properly, do it your fuckin' self.'*

"Right. There's gonna be some serious talkin' once this shit is sorted out. When that skinny bitch comes back," Faz had no doubt that she would; "Don't let her leave!"

All this was coming over the air and Lyla could hear it. There was nothing that could be done about that other than Sacha's offering reassurance to the terrified girl.

"You're safe now, honey. We've got you."

Leaning over, with a steadying hand on Lyla's arm, Sacha saw again that the momentary terror at hearing Faz's voice was subsiding quickly into what looked like rage. The girl emanated anger like a white heat. An idea surfaced. Sacha covered the camera on her phone and waited for the screen to demand the code. Entering it, the teams GPS locators glowed; she looked to see who was where. Satisfied, she gave Tom directions, aiming for where two of those dots were converging. Tom, mystified, complied.

"Relax, honey." Sacha was talking quietly to Lyla.

"You're mad right now, aren't you? I can't let you hold onto that; it will eat you up, I've been there. I know. Time for some payback."

Faz slammed the door behind him. Having to get dressed had pissed him off, having to leave the house had raised his level of 'pissed off' to hopping mad. His Friday night was going to shit and now he was having to fix someone else's fuck up. Storming to the car, he smashed the door shut and furiously started the engine. Gunning the big motor, he reversed the Range Rover from the drive, hearing sharp grit strike the underside. "Fuck!"

Ramming the lever into 'D', Faz floored the pedal, a mistake given the power beneath the bonnet, the car fishtailing. Calming himself, he eased off the accelerator, grinding his teeth in frustration. His destination was only a few minutes away. En route, any apprehension he felt about his appearance, and its effect on the girls was dispelled. The heavily tinted privacy windows would give the guys time to bundle the girls into the car before any sense of something wrong hit them. There would be no fuckin' around tonight. Faz was mad, pissed off at everything and everyone. The girls would pay first and if they got fucked up or squealed too loud, they'd go in the cellar for disposal later. Badboy had started this fuck up. He'd be answering for that.

Faz parked at the agreed rendezvous. He couldn't see shit through the side windows or rear and was reduced to leaning forwards, trying to improve the panorama.

He didn't believe it at first, but the slight motion of the Range Rover and the sound was unmistakeable. *'Some fucker was keying his paintwork!'* He roared and heaving on the lever, swung his door open so hard, it bounced back on the hinges, momentarily and untidily halting his exit. That served only to increase his rage.

"You cunt!"

As far as his bulk would allow, he leapt from the car, ready to deal out some serious damage to whoever had been dumb enough to fuck with his 'Range'.

The door had barely closed behind him when something black and hard came out of the darkness and his nose erupted from a stinging blast of violence. The taste of blood the last thing he remembered before taking a knuckled blow to the side of his head. His brain knocked off centre, it floated rapidly across his skull and hit other side, creating confusion and disorientation. He felt himself propelled sideways, colliding with the implacable steel of the door rim. Then came a rigid blow to his throat compromising his oesophagus, larynx, vocal cords, and trachea. Instantaneously he lost the ability to breathe or stand and he fell sideways to the ground, his bulk taking a moment to settle. Still conscious, he tried to speak, but couldn't. He tried to stand but it was useless, then to his surprise felt someone helping him to his feet. His breath came in ragged gasps, his throat constricted, burning.

"You're up girl."

Lyla blinked. She'd watched the events of the last couple of minutes, terrified as Faz's Range had screeched to the kerb. Seen the guy key it along the length of the car, then when Faz got out, seen him slammed to the deck.

She felt more than heard her door open and the social worker lean in and take her by the arm. "D'you ever see what happens when a guy gets kicked in the balls?"

The woman's eyes held an invitation, a sense of mischief that Lyla hadn't seen before, but she remembered the word 'payback' and got out of the car.

She watched as the woman spoke briefly to what were now two guys in black, faces covered by balaclavas, supporting a very dazed Faz, his legs an inverted V, trying to stay upright. Whatever she'd said, the two guys had nodded. The woman turned to face her, then beckoned her over. Then she understood.

Lyla launched herself at the fat man, the greasy man, the evil, stinking excuse for a man and with some velocity, delivered a kick so well aimed, so deliberate, so forceful that Faz squealed like the pig he was. His arms pinned by the two men in black, Faz couldn't even grasp the parts that hurt. The densely packed nerve endings unprotected by muscle or bone screamed and transmitted signals down the shared nerves between his scrotum and abdomen. His knees buckled and his captors struggled to hold his dead weight.

One of the guys leaned forward and whispered. "Go on, one more, you know you want to."

Lyla didn't need asking twice, she remembered those things on her chin, slapping against her ass, in her face, being encouraged to tickle them. Well, this was one tickle Faz was never going to forget. Using every muscle from her buttocks, thigh, and calf she leaned back and with the memory of a thousand rapes, energised her right foot; kicking Faz with such force, he vomited. He felt something twist or break inside and passing out from the sheer agony of the second kick, collapsed to the ground, unable to breathe, think, or recover. He was a quivering pile of snot and pain.

"Did you have to kick him so hard?" One of the men chided. "We've got to pick the fucker up now."

"Sorry." Muttered Lyla, not a bit contrite. Then, "Not sorry."

The woman took her by the arm.

"Who the fook are you people?"

"I'm Sacha, the guy in the car is my husband, Tom."

"Not social workers then?" She was being gently led back to the waiting car. A sense of release having passed through her at giving Faz a kicking.

"No honey. Not even close." They drove away.

Between the three of them, James, Ollie, and Dave managed to lift and roll the unconscious fat man into the van. He was hooded, secured, jabbed and inert. His load provoking involuntary exhalations from Badboy and Eric, who had the misfortune to be underneath him.

"That just leaves Mo."

"Let's not forget our friendly, neighbourhood PCC." Ollie reiterated.

"Let's not." Replied James.

James and Ollie strolled casually to the front door. They'd donned stab vests beneath their windcheaters and their balaclavas were rolled up to look like beanies. They kept their faces down, camera aware. They had comms with Control and Dave, no buttons required, just speak, or listen.

Lyla had given them the layout of the house, such as she knew it. Victorian, double bay fronted, the ground floor was a hallway, leading the length of the house to a kitchen at the back. About five yards inside the front door, left and right, were doors that led to reception rooms. The rapes took place mainly upstairs, in four bedrooms. A bathroom and toilet above the kitchen. Surprisingly, the front door was on the latch.

'That would be Faz leaving in a huff and not checking.' Thought James, leading.

It took no more than the turn of an old, round, brass knob to get them in. If the spices on the street were an indication of the area, the aroma inside was confirmation. But there was an underlay of unwashed humanity, musty carpets, curtains, bedding in need of a change. An overall sense of a cesspit requiring emptying. They pulled down their balaclava's.

Dave's voice drifted informatively into their earpieces.

"One downstairs, room on your left. One up, front right bedroom." The thermal images Dave viewed were clear. But there was an anomaly.

"Guys. I'm getting a cluster, it's faint but underground. There must be a cellar."

"Roger that." James breathed. He looked across to Ollie, who shrugged at the news. "We do this quiet." Ollie nodded.

Mo had taken a call from one of his drivers. 'The streets don't feel right.' He'd said. Looking around the room of which he was the sole occupant, even slightly befuddled by weed, Mo had to agree. There had never, ever been a time when one or more of his mates wasn't present. Mo hadn't survived this long, doing what he did, without listening to his inner genie. He always kept a knife handy, some of the girls 'liked' to be cut, or have it held to their throat. He slipped it under his right leg. Just in case.

In the living room, Mo appeared spaced. Even the sight of two masked men did no more than cause a fit of the giggles. "Ninja!" He blurted, cheerfully. "Fuckin' ninja."

This was going to be easy. Whilst they were concentrating on how to lift the fat man from sofa, they didn't notice the giggling had stopped or see the knife in Mo's hand until it was too late, the narrowing of Mo's eyes the first clue something was amiss. Steel flashed and found the edge of James's stab vest, sinking into the soft space just above his left armpit. Reflexively James head butted Mo, blood spurting freely from the contact. His nose flattened, Mo subsided, grunting, back onto the sofa, the knife dropping to the floor.

"Shit! Fuck! Bollocks! How did that happen?"

James was checking his wound, the incident registered but the pain not yet forthcoming.

Ollie pulled James's hand away and took a close look, his booted foot pressing down on Mo. "You'll be fine. Just a scratch."

"Scratch?" James hissed, through clenched teeth, then ignoring the wound for the time being, got back on mission.

"Get Dave in here and that fat bastard up and bundled."

He used his free hand to staunch the bleeding. Another check showed that it wasn't going to be fatal, more of a hindrance. Dave entered and glancing first at James, then lent Ollie a hand in none to gently assisting Mo to join his friends in the van which, as Ollie had foretold, was starting to get a bit crowded.

Ollie returned with a field dressing and sitting James down, got to work.

"Careful, you fucking moron!"

"Don't be a fanny." Chided Ollie, as he swiftly and expertly set about James's shoulder. "There goes your record. Now you have a scar. Can't wait to hear how this one gets told around the swinging lamp."

James chuckled. "Years of tackling professionals and I get fucked up by a fat man on a sofa. You done?"

"Yep." Said Ollie, inspecting his handiwork, then the room, scuzzy and polluted.

"Hope your tetanus is up to date though." He raised an eyebrow to the stairs. "Now what?"

James was thoughtful. "I'm wondering about that one."

They'd had the feed from Lyla's phone throughout, heard the shouting, the frustration, and irritation as the occupants slowly unravelled. They knew Mayfield was waiting in the bedroom, they hoped he was either drunk, coked up, or asleep. The latter unlikely, due to the drugs.

"He's quiet for the time being. Let's see if we can find this cellar. Eyes open."

James stood, testing the movement in his shoulder. It was starting to hurt; he hoped adrenalin would take care of that.

The door wasn't hidden, unobtrusive, except for the padlock; easily ignored and overcome by splintering the old, dried out pine beneath the steel hasp.

"People never learn." Ollie observed.

Unlit save for the glow coming from the open door behind, they made their way carefully down a dusty, concrete staircase. Through the gloom, they heard increasing notes of panicked whimpering as they progressed. An ad hoc pathway had evolved between old bits of discarded furniture, clothing, bikes, the detritus suburban living so they followed it, walking carefully towards the sound. They smelt it before seeing it, a locked cage, medieval, filthy, and stinking of human waste. Four occupants. Huddled, cold and frightened. The whites of their eyes large.

"Jesus."

Over his mic, James briefed the others on what the cellar 'anomaly' had been. He'd decided that as much as he'd like to do something about it, the girls would have to stay where they were until an official rescue could be mounted, their condition and location positive proof of what the purpose of the house was. He finished his sitrep with an instruction for Dave.

"Bring a syringe."

As Police and Crime Commissioner, Mayfield couldn't simply disappear so a different approach would be needed. They'd see what they found when they got upstairs and then decide what that approach would be.

They crept upward. In the top corridor, a glance showed only one door with the giveaway crack of light where it almost met the floor.

"Ready?" James whispered.

"Watch out for professional knife fighters." Ollie bantered.

James silenced him with an index finger to his lips then mouthed three words, each punctuated with a stiff finger to his mate's chest. *'You. Massive. Bellend.'* Then jerked his thumb towards the bedroom door.

Mayfield's status within the group offered some assurance that he would be the room's sole occupant and on swinging the door open wide, this was confirmed. What was also immediately apparent, was that he'd got bored waiting.

He was seated on the edge of the bed, mansplaining, his trousers around his ankles and his cock in his hand, eyes riveted on a tv screen. His first thought was to start shouting.

"How dare you! Haven't you heard of kno…"

It was the work of only a few minutes to rearrange the man and his surroundings.

"Stuart. Did you get all of that?"

"Every word." Came back over James's earpiece.

"Mayfield's still upstairs but out of it, we've doped him. We've had to leave the girls in the cellar. Are you thinking what I'm thinking?"

"I am. Leave. I'll make the call." Ames closed down the discussion and dialled Arham.

Arham

In the cold light of day, DCI Arham Khan was a happy man. Stuart had called with information and an address. A search of that address had revealed the mess he was now in the process of making sense of.

In the cellar his teams had found four young girls. Imprisoned, beaten, starved, half naked and each had a story to tell. Upstairs, they'd been astonished to discover their PCC, Peter Mayfield. He was asleep in front of a tv with his trousers around his ankles. The home movie he'd dozed off to was one in which he had a starring role along with what were very clearly, underage, and unwilling girls. Drugs paraphernalia and further child porn completed the tableau. There was no sign of any other occupants. Mayfield was now in cells down at the station and Arham couldn't wait to see what his lawyers came up with.

A property search revealed that the owner was one Fazawi Alam, a prominent local businessman who'd been on Arham's radar for some considerable time. Mayfield's presence was all the explanation Arham had needed for how elusive Faizal Alam had been. Alam could not be found but criminal charges were stacking up in Arham's mind and it seemed to him, that with the profound absence of anyone else to take the fall, Mayfield's would be spectacular.

There was no way something this big, someone this big, caught literally with his pants down and surrounded by the most damning evidence could be ignored, not this time. The satisfaction of that aside, Arham was optimistic that for the time being at least, his streets would be a safer place, particularly for adolescent females.

Stuart had asked for discretion and he, Arham, would give it for now but knew he had questions for Ames later. The girls had talked animatedly about men dressed in black, wearing masks. On waking and when being questioned, Mayfield had said much the same.

Arham decided that for official purposes, whoever had been at work last night were his men, his initiative, brought together with the express purpose of breaking up these grooming gangs. The thought that his 'task force' existed might dissuade any more of these filthy fuckers sticking their heads above the parapet.

The Promise

The early morning drive back to Themis was undertaken in silence, Sacha deep in thought, Tom, weary and concentrating on the road. Lyla had rejected an offer to go home, saying there was nothing there she wanted, or needed.

On the premise that they couldn't simply abandon her, she had accompanied Tom and Sacha and was curled up on the back seat, emotionally drained and fast asleep. Sacha figured she had 24 hours to work on Tom.

Ames and the boys were the only one's involved in the next two phases, interrogation, and 'deportation'. This left her and Tom with time on their hands; time she intended to put to good use.

She recalled that first interview. How Lyla had the steel to fight back, despite her fear and misgivings. She knew the girl had a sharp intelligence. Reading between the lines of her school reports declared as much. She appeared to have bounced back remarkably well from her experiences. Perhaps because she'd had a hand in the downfall of the gang. Sacha didn't know, but if the girl needed a therapist, one would be found.

In her mind Sacha had mapped out a different ending to this girl's story, with the right support and with Tom on side, it could be done. She knew enough about Tom to know that he just needed an occasional nudge in the right direction…her direction. Sacha wasn't being selfish in this; it would do Tom good. Sacha also knew that sending Lyla back meant her future was uncertain, but most likely non-existent. Having fixed in her mind what needed to be done, Sacha set about figuring out how to achieve it. The road slipped darkly beneath their wheels. HQ was an hour away, daylight, an hour or so later.

A brief chat, "I need to talk to Tom." And an encouraging smile had managed to prise Lyla from Sacha's side. Revived by breakfast, Lyla was now with Dave, walking the grounds, dazed by the huge green space, staggered by the majesty of the big house. Fully occupied, at least for the time being.

Neil was in the workshop, grumbling about having to flush out the shit, piss and blood that decorated the deck of the van. The workshop area being completely level, he'd had to jack the front of the van up before sluicing the muck away down a nearby drain.

Bailey, James, and Ollie were in their small but well-equipped Med room where she properly cleaned, stitched, and dressed James's knife wound. Ollie looked on; offering unwanted advice, principally concerning the obvious dangers of approaching an old, fat man with a knife and how to avoid being stabbed. The gang of four were tucked away securely in the bunker, finding out how it feels to be caged.

Sacha had Tom cornered in a side office. It was time to go to work.

"We're done here, at least for now, we were brought in to play our part, we've done that but now we have a problem", she paused, "Lyla doesn't want to go back", another pause, "I don't want to send her back. She can come with us. Home."

"Are you off your head?"

"You go easy, Tom Hood. Hear me out."

"What about her parents? School? Other stuff." He felt his arguments weakening.

"Well, in the first instance," said Sacha. "She's sixteen in a few days. She gets to choose."

"Between what?" Asked Tom, wary of the answer. They already had a menagerie at home. A teenage creche was not on the top of his list of favourite things, despite his respect for the way the girl had handled herself.

"That's just it, isn't it, Tom? She's stuck between the devil and the deep blue sea. She's not going home, she said so herself. Where does that leave her? Her parents don't give a rat's ass and her school wasn't worth the name."

"You just said 'wasn't', why wasn't? That suggests she 'isn't' going back?" He was being pedantic, he knew.

"Tom. Sit down, please." Sacha patted the sofa, on the space by her side. She took Tom's hand and locked her eyes on his.

"When we sat in that school, we made that girl a promise. We, not me. Now I don't care where or why that promise was made; it stands. Whatever problems you think there are, they're nothing compared to what that girl's had to face. She helped us close those assholes down, what she did saved the lives of four girls that we know of, and God knows how many more we don't. For all we know there are other scumbags out there, waiting for her to reappear 'n take her down. She's smart, she's tough and she needs a break. Right now, Tom Hood, you 'n me are that break. She deserves a shot."

Tom was concerned that Sacha was speaking from the heart, not the head. But playing Devil's Advocate didn't feel right. He'd developed a respect for Lyla but the real threat that she'd been psychologically damaged loomed large in his mind. In every other respect, Sacha was right, Lyla's history, went against her but the sheer guts she'd shown going back into that house had impressed. But there was another issue. One that had to be voiced.

"She's not…"

"I know, Tom. She's not Ellen. Never could be, never will be. But there is a life here that we can change. We're a team, Tom

Hood. The best I've ever known. If she can get to know how good it feels to be part of something like that then maybe we get to leave something behind."

Tom recognised Sacha's determination, and that fact that he might not be forgiven if he didn't at least let her try. And a promise was a promise. With some reservations, the decision made, he got behind it.

In the Bunker

In the Ops room, Ames and the boys faced the new issue. Human trafficking. Lyla had hinted at it; the caged girls had added to the theory, but they needed to know for sure, and there was only one way to confirm it.

They walked together to the bunker. Passing Dave and Lyla on the way.

"We could do worse than letting her soften them up." Ollie grinned, as they passed through the green, steel door.

Ames felt uncomfortable in the balaclava. Not because it itched, but it's paramilitary connotations. He was more used to an interview room and the polite formalities of interrogation.

"Who's first?"

The diminutive stature of the cuffed, hooded figure identified it as Badboy. He came shuffling in between James and Ollie, clearly shaken by his overnight experience, and the uncertain nature of his situation. They parked him on a steel chair, a bright light shining directly facing it, and secured him with plasticuffs, his hands behind his back, his ankles to the chair legs.

Ames straightened the laptop, a little bit of OCD to camouflage his uncertainty. Then reminded himself what the subject in front of him was guilty of. He spoke, his voice disguised by software installed on his computer.

"Take it off." The alien sound of his own voice boomed, echoing around the bunker. For their purposes, the sinister edge added another dimension to their questions, what wouldn't Ames have given for a set up like this, back in the day.

His hood whipped away, Badboy blinked rapidly, then screwed his eyes shut, the light hurting his eyes. These fuckers had snatched him, drugged him, and messed with his world. His face hurt. The brief glimpse he'd caught as his hood came off was not reassuring. This wasn't legal and they made no pretence that it was. It had to be a gang; looking to take over their patch. That made his future unpredictable and the likely prospect of violence, imminent. Police pussies Badboy could handle, all it took was a decent lawyer and denial, but if he was going to come out on the other side of this, a different approach would be needed.

"Hey guys. You don't need all this shit." He tried very hard to be matey, companionable, trying to the keep the whine out of his voice. "Just ask."

Slowly, in the silence that followed, Badboy allowed his eyes to adjust. Beyond the painful light, he could make out a desk with three seated figures. All hooded. That was a good sign. They didn't want to be identified, that meant his chances of survival had jumped up a notch or two. He grew in confidence.

"Guys. I get it. Faz had it good for a while but got sloppy. You're the new kids on the block. Cut me loose. We can talk. I know his operation inside out. I can help."

"Trafficking."

Badboy flinched as the magic voice echoed around the room. He felt like he was in Oz with the Wizard and two flyin' monkeys. *'Weird, man. Weird.'*

"Come again?"

"Get rid of him," That booming echo again. "Bring the next one in."

Badboy panicked. "No! Wait! Trafficking. Yeah. What about it?" If anyone was getting out of this, it was going to be him. Fuck solidarity, the others would drop him straight in the shit and leave him bare ass naked, he needed to get in first, be of value.

"Badboy."

That fuckin' voice again. It was grating on his nerves, unsettling him. Those two silent fuckers either side of The Wizard scared the shit out of him, this didn't look like an interview panel, didn't feel like one, either.

"Just tell us what you know. Don't make anything up. Don't lie. We'll know if you do, and we won't be happy."

If they wanted 'happy', Badboy was their man. He laid it out.

"None of it was my idea, man. Faz set it up. You know about the girls, right?"

Of course they did. That's why he was here.

"So trafficking, used up ones were bundled and sold off to a connection in Turkey. We'd truck 'em out and get rid. They're worth money, bruv." He hoped that last sentence would pique their interest and expected they'd ask about the cash value. They didn't.

"How many?"

"What?"

"How many!?" The voice boomed, louder.

Badboy sensed a change in the room. A new threat. Were they mad at him because he'd asked the question? Or was it what they'd done with the girls? It was a crucial point. They were either displaying impatience, which he could deal with, or worse, actually gave a shit what happened to the girls.

"Dunno man. It's been goin' on for years but lately, there's been maybe eight. There are four more, due out soon, in the cellar at his place." He added, hopefully. Eager to prove his worth.

"When were the eight girls moved?"

"Four got moved months ago, man. The second batch went last week."

"Those numbers are too big. That many local girls go missing, too many questions."

"They ain't all local, bruv. We pick 'em up from all over the place, London, Liverpool, Manchester, the big cities. Runaways, mostly. Faz just added one of ours when she got used up or started mouthing off. That's it."

"So Faz is the main man, right? What about Eric and Mo?"

Badboy snorted. "Eric don't know shit. He 'aint no use to you. Just went there to fuck the young 'uns 'n be the big man."

"And Mo?"

"Taxis. That's all."

"No, Badboy. Not all." The voice was low now, knowing. "Tell us about Mo."

"Ok! Ok!" There was a time for loyalty, usually in the good times. Something in the back of Badboy's mind told him these dudes were bad, real bad. But he couldn't get a handle on their motives and was starting not to care.

"Ok. The taxis bit is true. But Mo's likes 'em young. Likes 'em quiet. He's not a good Moslem, he does booze 'n drugs."

"And you are, I suppose."

Badboy shrugged. "Non practising, bruv."

"Anything else?"

Badboy decided deflecting attention from his part would be worth exploring. He knew about Mo.

"He's got two kids, bruv. Girls." Badboy let the implication hang in the air.

"Keep talking."

"Used to fuck 'em. But they grew up. Kicked back. Told his missus."

Ames swallowed a build-up of bile.

"You know this?"

"Got pissed one night 'n blabbed a bit. Seems his missus was only good for breedin' him some kids to fuck, girls or boys, didn't matter which. That's it."

Ames had heard as much as he wanted to about Mo.

"And Faz?

"I can't, bruv. He's family."

"Take him out."

"No! Wait!" To survive this, Badboy reckoned it was time to look after number one. Faz was an old man, anyway. These boys were serious and Badboy wanted to go places. If he 'fessed up, chances are he'd be useful.

"Waddya need?"

"I want more, tell us about the route, the destination, names."

"Same routine each time, just before they leave I gotta hose 'em down. The price gets agreed on pick up 'n they gotta look decent." Badboy's voice dropped, sensing his usefulness ended with his knowledge. "After that, I don't know."

"Right." Said The Wizard, in that distorted voice. "Take him back to the cage. Bring Faz out."

Faz was in the dark. He knew they'd already taken Badboy, had heard the echo of conversation, interrogation. He knew also that he was in company in this cage. Mo, snuffling and snoring, still wasted from last night and Eric. Fuckin' useless Eric, babbling and blubbing, Faz could smell stale piss and hoped that whatever that puddle was that he was sitting in, it wasn't that.

He heard footsteps and shuffling, Badboy, he supposed. He'd heard the pitch and whine of Badboy's voice over the echoes and just knew he'd spilled his guts.

He wondered how much damage had been done to his operation. It all added to the cost of buying his way out of here. He figured his nose was busted, tasting, and smelling blood. He couldn't swallow without pain and wondered if he could still talk, he grunted, testing. His head throbbed from a punch. Someone, somewhere, would pay.

He heard a key tumble in a metal lock and sensed Badboy getting into position. Hands gripped him on either side, and he was unkindly lifted and made to walk, unable to stand straight, stooped from the pain in his balls. Every step he took an exercise in agony. He wondered bleakly if they'd ever work again and when he replayed the image of her skinny face, when she'd dared to look him in the eye as she kicked him, vowed that that little bitch would know the meaning of pain.

"So, you're the man."

Strapped in the chair, Faz had waited, heard people moving, had twitched wondering from which direction any violence might be arriving. Then came the words, in that deep, off world address. It was a statement, not a question and Faz now had his answer to the strange echoing noises he'd heard earlier.

"I need medical treatment."

"Don't hold your breath." The voice was flat, loud, and unsettling. Like being held prisoner in a spaceship.

Faz shrugged. He'd get his doc to sort him once he got back.

"How much?"

"How much what?" The voice queried.

"Money. Dumb fuck. How much do you want."

"You can't buy your way out of this, and you can forget Mayfield. He has problems of his own."

'Fuck!' That meant they'd been to the house. *'What else was going on?'* "I don't know no Mayfield."

"Well, he's your Deputy Mayor, and Police and Crime Commissioner. Useful guy to know."

Faz slumped, wondering what else they knew. "Get to the point."

"It's over Faz. You're wiped out. Mayfield is talking up a storm, your 'fun house' is being gone over by proper policemen and as for your cellar, well, it wasn't wine you kept down there, was it?"

Above all else Faz was a pragmatist and he let his brain do a quick rewrite. He'd have to bring his retirement plan forward is all. England was fucked as far as he was concerned. It was time to go. Once he was out of here, he'd get his ass to Turkey. The set-up there was sweet. He allowed himself an inner smile and continued bargaining.

"So, you don't want money, but there's a price for everything, mystery man. What do you want? The cost we can work out later."

"Your trafficking route. All of it."

Faz felt a stab of alarm. That fuckin' asshole Badboy, had jeopardised his retirement plan. He wasn't lettin' that go. No way.

"Not happenin'."

"We'll see." Faz was hooded and taken back to the cage. It still stank of piss. Faz tried to find a dry spot.

Air Time

Ames needed to see Christian. Having tested their theory, James and Ollie had outlined their preferred method for 'deporting' the grooming gang and some specific permissions were required. He needed the jet. The boys had looked it over and declared it fit for purpose. Not necessarily as the FAA or Christians insurance company might define the proper use for an executive jet, but fit, nevertheless. Ames had modified his 'no killing' rule to accept the risk of an accidental death. The animals caged in the bunker had gone beyond the realms of criminal behaviour and so, like The Twins, were a special case.

In shirtsleeves and needing a haircut, Christian was engrossed in his screens. "Sit down, Stuart, please. I just need a moment."

As good as his word, a moment was all it took. He smiled briefly at his monitor, then looked up and addressed Ames.

"How lovely to see you." Christian seemed genuinely pleased. "I trust all is well?"

"Yes. Thanks, Peter." This was a big ask, Ames hesitated. "It's something of a courtesy call, actually."

"Go on."

Ames chose his words carefully. Despite having had a free hand with Themis and funds, he wasn't certain that 'whatever you need' applied to the big, expensive toys.

"Can we borrow your jet?"

"Jet? Oh! Of course! Yes. The jet."

Christian arched an eyebrow, thoughtfully. "Should I ask why?"

"It's probably best not to. We'll try to bring it back in one piece."

"It's to be part of your current operation?"

Ames had kept Christian in the broader picture, again, as a matter of courtesy. Christian had wished him every success, and enquired from time to time on how matters were progressing. The outcome of the operation clearly gaining interest up here, on the top floor.

"The end game if you like. We have them, we'd like to ensure they don't come back."

Christian leaned forward, steepling his fingers, as was his habit when being sincere.

"Stuart, whatever is on these grounds is yours to do with as you please. It's just a jet. You don't need my permission to use it."

Ames knew that 'just a jet' cost upwards of 60 million USD. A frightening number. He was reminded again that Christian dealt in the stratosphere of finance. He was still getting used to 'budget' being a thing of the past.

"Do you need the pilots? The aircraft needs two, you know."

Ames did. But not Christian's civilians. Bailey had contacted an acquaintance, Wes, ex RAF and formerly of The Queens Flight but more significantly, ex Joint Special Forces Aviation Wing, which maintained and operated a covert fleet of aircraft specifically for secretive and usually hazardous ops, attracting only pilots of the highest calibre. His service recently completed, Wes had been sat on his thumbs contracting out to the rich, powerful, and occasionally obnoxious on flights of fancy. Bailey knew her man and his low boredom threshold, and tempted him with the nature of the flight, low and off the books.

"Well, I've nothing on this week." Had been the jovial response. "But we're not cleaning the toilets."

Well versed with jet aircraft, Wes concurred that while technically the G550 could be flown with just a single pilot, this was reserved for emergencies only and he had just the man in mind to serve as co-pilot. Bailey had their fliers en route.

"Probably best not to." Admitted Ames. "Not this time."

"Anything else you need."

The aircraft issue resolved, Ames broached another, more sensitive one.

"Nothing that won't keep but Sacha Hood has expressed a desire to meet you."

"Ah. Yes." Christian was back on uncertain ground now, embarrassment and shame the root cause.

"It'll be ok, Peter. She's a remarkable woman, capable of many things, including forgiveness, I think."

"Still," said Christian. "She was the child's mother."

Ames corrected him. Understanding Christians inner turmoil, and sense of guilt. "You'll need to start using Ellen's name, Peter. And I think meeting Sacha would do you both good."

Ames had seen for himself that meetings between victims and perpetrators could produce positive outcomes. He felt for Christian and hoped that some inner peace might ease the man. He also knew that Sacha needed this. He was certain that a meeting might offer peace of mind to them both and hoped that this might bring Christian out of his self-imposed exile, here, upstairs.

Christian, often stood at his window on the world, looking outward while studying inward. Occasionally, he caught glimpses of Tom and Sacha. Perhaps it was time, however unready he was. Setting that aside, he had a question for Ames.

"Stuart?" He paused, this was a personal matter and he thought of himself as a deeply impersonal man.

"My ex-wife?"

Ames looked up, engaging with Christian.

"Um…I've had a communication from my lawyers. Some months ago, in fact just after you picked up the reins, she appears to have been involved in an embarrassing episode."

"So I heard." Replied Ames, non-committaly.

"Um…anything I should know?"

Ames studied the man in front of him, he'd decided some time ago that Christian was a decent man, simply out of his depth socially and emotionally. Dealing with Ms. Hutchison had given him a deep sense of satisfaction, freeing the man in front of him one facet of that. He chose his words carefully.

He smiled, saying, "Themis, Sir. Her symbol is the scales of justice. Call it divine intervention."

Deportation

The aircraft was a Gulfstream G550. It needed a minimum of 1800 metres to take off, they had 2.5km. Christian had moved it to the estate months ago once the runway had been made serviceable. His brief forays into the wider world were infrequent, but always private. It could carry up to 19 passengers, depending on the cabin configuration which in this case, was for six, seated in comfort, but more to the point, had a cargo door that once under 12000ft; when cabin pressure and oxygen wasn't an issue, could be opened in flight; a feature Ollie had mentioned to James when contemplating what to do with the grooming gang. Years of experience of exiting numerous aircraft types while at altitude had inspired an idea, and this was the theory they had tested and suggested to Ames. They were looking forward to its practical application.

The Gulfstream had a range of 6,750 nautical miles. Their ultimate destination was 3,620 miles away but as they didn't intend to land, their pilots, Wes and Juddy, though indicating a readiness to exploit the aircrafts capabilities to the full, had recommended that to be certain of a full return trip, rather than what they termed as 'suffering a terminal aircraft event', meant refuelling somewhere en route. Cyprus was four hours and 2300 miles away, and friendly, the second leg to the 'drop off' a little over 2000 miles and decidedly unfriendly. They'd refuel in Cyprus, there and back. Just to be on the safe side.

Ames had insisted on accompanying them, stating his recently acquired command of Greek might prove useful They couldn't argue with that and anyway, he was the Boss. The grooming gang were at the rear, trussed, hooded, clustered uncomfortably on the floor beneath a spider net secured with tie down rings and stud fittings to redundant seat tracks. They were going nowhere and had no in-flight catering.

Up front, Wes fully tenanted the pilot's seat, burly, jovial, and missing only the handlebar moustache. Beside him as co-pilot, Juddy, of comparable build and disposition. Their careers in aviation had followed similar paths and they had history sharing a cockpit. They ran through the pre-flight checks conscientiously, their customary banter reserved for punctuating the inevitable in-flight monotony. Checks complete, Wes leaned back in his seat and gave a thumbs up through the open door.

"Ready when you are, old lad."

His passengers settled and belted, Wes's meaty hand found the throttles, and eased them forwards. The Twin Rolls Royce B710 engines roared, the jet accelerating, and rotated skyward.

Four uneventful hours later, they landed to take on fuel. Larnaca International Airport opened in 1975 on the site of an old

British airbase, Nicosia having ceased to operate after Turkey invaded in 1974. By 2009, tourism outgrew the original structure, so a new passenger terminal was built next door, leaving the old airport complex for cargo, private jets, and light planes.

If your only purpose was to refuel, a transit visa was all that was necessary, any checks minimal, disembarking optional, a quick turnaround the favoured outcome. Bailey had done the paperwork; Ames did the talking. An hour later, they were airborne again. The aircraft flew high and wide over Syria, Azerbaijan, skirted the northern border of Afghanistan and then looped south, over the Hindu Kush. They navigated to the top end of the Shiber Pass. A long feature running roughly North to South and 9800 above sea level. They needed to depressurise the cabin and had 2000ft to play with. Wes got them steady at 11,500. Both pilots knew what was about to happen, having given technical advice on how to achieve it. They strapped themselves in and wore oxygen, just in case.

"Time to offload." Said Ollie, flatly. They pulled on their balaclavas.

Beneath the spider net, and the hoods, the gang had evidently heard the statement and some agitation was evident. Ames had no use for any of them bar Faz, who still retained the information they needed, somehow still believing he still had options. It was time to disabuse him of the notion. Time to renegotiate. Ames came to the rear of the Gulfstream, masked, crouching beside the net and the four men beneath it. James and Ollie tugged the sacks from their heads. They squinted on coming into the light, then adjusting, scanned wildly for information.

"Just a short speech for you boys, before you go." Greeted Ames. "This is our take on a new method of deportation. No lawyers involved. No last minute ECHR pyjama judges to step in. It's just us."

He pointed to a canvas pile of parachutes and watched as three confused and apprehensive faces did a double take. Faz appeared defiant, perhaps confident that whatever was going to happen next, throwing people from aeroplanes only happened in the movies. Ames carried on with their reality check in a flat tone, he wanted that information and they needed to know how far he was prepared to go to get it.

"You've no papers, nothing to say who or what you are. You've no money." He paused, allowing their suddenly stateless and impoverished predicament to register.

"I'd avoid the locals. If you know your Kipling, which I doubt, you'll know why. Assuming you land in one piece, I'd head south. You do know how to figure out which way is south? Anyway, that's Pakistan. Not sure quite how far it is. We don't want to see you trying to get back, and we'll know if you do. Any questions?"

Their presence in an aircraft, the pile of parachutes and talk of surviving a landing abruptly came together, though not simultaneously. Eric was first to put the organise the pieces into a complete, unnerving picture.

Eric howled. "What about me? I'm white!"

"Ah." Said Ames, softly.

"It's the new age, Eric. We believe in equal opportunities for all. If you lie down with dogs, you'll get up with fleas." Ames stood and nodded to James and Ollie.

Grasping at straws Johnson tried one last thing.

"I've served!"

"No, Eric. You fucking haven't." Said James, flatly, disapproving of stolen valour. "We do background checks, you moron."

"Who's first?" Asked Ollie, cheerfully. "Any of you boys used a parachute before? Oh. And by the way, we only have three."

There were no volunteers. Somehow, against all evidence to the contrary, they still wanted to believe this was all a bluff. In their cage, they'd quietly discussed who these people were and decided they were Government, not rivals. Who else had private jets? No-one was gonna get thrown out of a plane.

"Fuck you." Spat Faz.

James and Ollie secured themselves with harnesses. Ollie was to do the heavy lifting, James's shoulder something of a niggle. Up front, unhappy at the prospect of the aircraft's integrity being deliberately breached, Ames regained his seat and pulled the belt as tight as comfort would allow, then tightened it some more.

Ollie opened the cargo door, it wasn't big, perhaps 1.5 square metres but the impact within the cloistered aircraft was instant.

The proximity of the jet engines became immediately apparent, manifested as a terrifying, macerating, constant scream. There was an instant chill as cold air buffeted the interior, anything not strapped down instantly airborne, stray tissues, polystyrene cups making random circuits. Clothing flapped and hair whipped around faces. The boys were used to it, competent parachutists as a matter of course, but their passengers weren't.

'*Who the fuck opened airplane doors mid-flight?!*'

To emphasise their point; that this was really happening, wordlessly, James nodded, and Ollie pulled a wriggling, now hysterical Eric from beneath the net.

"Don't make me give you a slap."

Having to shout to be heard, Ollie hinted at violence unless the man calmed down, a strategy that changed nothing. Eric was a howling, petrified, maniac. Reaching behind, Ollie took a prepared hypodermic and jabbed the foaming man in the arm. In his unbalanced state, Eric didn't feel the needle, but his nervous system felt it effects and shut down. Letting him fall limply to the floor, Ollie strapped a parachute to his back, attached a temporary static line, then cut his plasticuffs. A chance at survival. Giving the remaining three an evil, meaningful look, he sat on his haunches and maintaining eye contact with the others, pushed an unconscious Eric out of the aircraft.

The attitude inside the cabin changed instantly. Not to the point where any of its reluctant occupants felt like volunteering to be next, but one of silent, simple, wide-eyed panic.

"Two left boys." Said Ollie, holding up a parachute. "But three of you. Who's it gonna be?"

"What the fuck you doin', bruv!?" Badboy got verbal. "We got rights! This 'aint civilised! Fuck, man! Eric!?"

"Probably landed by now." Said Ollie. "Safe and sound. Might even have found a boyfriend."

He grabbed Mo's leg. "The knifeman cometh." He said to no-one in particular.

The clutching hand galvanised the fat man but trussed, he was unable to struggle free. His face reddened and veins stood out on his face and neck, he was spluttering, incoherent. He wasn't the only one. True panic had set in under the net and now free of it, Mo was becoming unmanageable. Ollie grabbed him and stuck another hypo up close and personal to the overwrought man's face.

"You want this?"

Mo whimpered, "I got a wife and kids."

"Big mistake, Mo, mentioning them. You think we don't know what you do to your kids? Your own kids!"

Mo, his hands still cuffed and unable to beg in any other way, fell to his knees, bowing until his forehead touched the floor, pleading.

Ollie held up the parachute and grasping the man's hair, looked down at his face.

"It's now or never Mo. Your choice, personally I don't give a shit if you wear it or not."

Something clicked in his head and Mo limply accepted whatever was coming. Ollie quickly finished preparing him and he followed Eric, letting out a thin, despairing wail as he exited.

"Is that a classic example of the Doppler Effect?" Asked Ollie, casually, of no-one in particular.

With Mo's departure, the chaos level reduced. Faz and Badboy having witnessed the simplicity of what was sure to be coming their way, mute in horror.

"And then there were two." Said Ollie, holding the last of the chutes.

Badboy looked frantically across at Faz, then the empty spaces left by Eric and Mo; then, at the last, remaining parachute. Faz wasn't responding to events, frozen by disbelief and fear.

"Me!" Screamed Badboy. "Fuck you! I'll go. What kind of fuckin' animals are you!?"

Ollie knelt beside the tethered Badboy. His man bun, free of tie, had long disintegrated and now fell over his sweating, contorted face.

"A fine question, Badboy. Coming from something like you and your mates. How did you like the cage? Nicer than the one we found some girls in. And as far as this goes?"

He lifted the parachute to Badboy's eye level. "We're giving you a better chance than you ever gave those kids."

"Wait!" Screamed Faz, elementary maths causing a rapid awakening to his desperate circumstances. "I'll tell you! Just give me that 'chute!"

"I'm listening." Said James, indicating to Ollie that the new noises coming from a now betrayed and overwrought Badboy needed sorting. Ollie gagged him.

Faz's story had the ring of truth and was electronically checked. It was all there, or at least appeared to be. How the trafficking had begun simply as a practical and profitable solution to the problem of what to do with used up girls. How they were moved and where they were sent. Satisfied that in the time they had they'd got as much from Faz as they could, Ames nodded to James and Ollie, who prepped him for departure.

Strapping the parachute on was simply done but the closer they edged him to the exit, the more clear, blue sky opened up, the harder it was to haul the heavy, protesting man to the edge. Finally, James had a word.

"Faz. You're going. Now we could knock you out, which would make life easier for us, but landing could be a problem for you or…you get on with it. It's your call."

Sweating, recalling the exit of his two erstwhile conspirators, Faz succumbed to the inevitable. His pride though, what was left of it, prompted parting words.

"This 'aint fuckin' over. You're dead."

"Fuck off, Faz." James placed a booted foot in the small of the fat man's back and pushed. He went out in a tumble.

Ollie took the gag from Badboy's mouth. He coughed, spitting. Then pleaded, "You're not pushing me out, not without a parachute. You're not gonna do that, are you, bruv?"

Ollie knelt beside the cowering spiv. A masked menace. "I've never liked you, Badboy. If it was up to me, you'd have been first out of the door. But we're not killers, not unless pushed. Stand up."

The fourth parachute was produced. Badboy's relief as he was being prepped came out in a series of 'Thank you's.' Not a bad conversion from ten minutes ago, before watching his mates take a dive.

Taking Badboy's travesty of a watch from a pocket, Ollie dangled it from its strap. A flicking motion sent it out through the cargo hatch. "Time flies." He said. Badboy had long since re-evaluated his priorities but nevertheless, couldn't help but follow the arc of the tacky timepiece as it exited.

"Don't come back." James said…and pushed. Badboy fell into the blue.

Shutting the cargo door and securing it, James went forward to talk to the pilots.

"Thanks guys. Nice work. You can take us back now."

"Thank fuck for that." Juddy muttered beneath the oxygen mask. There was a palpable sense of relief in the cockpit as the aircraft gained speed and altitude. They'd been close to stalling and too low for comfort.

James returned the cabin, offering a thumbs up. "Going home."

Ollie, surveying the empty spider net and the freshly stained carpet beneath it. Wrinkled his nose and exhaling noisily, performed an amdram wave of a hand in front of his face.

"Gonna need a clean before we give it back." He said, cheerfully.

"But it's not over yet, is it?" Ames said, musing, mulling over the information Faz had finally given up.

"That's your call, Boss." James replied.

Ollie piped up. "Turkey's nice, this time of year, I'm told."

They'd been on the return leg for perhaps an hour. James had noticed Ames looking reflectively to the rear of the aircraft, to where the groomers had been and was more taciturn than was usual. Ollie was stretched out beside him dozing so James moved forwards, taking a seat alongside their clearly troubled boss.

"How do you two cope?"

Ames was shell shocked. The description of what the boys intended for the gang had been sterile when discussed in the confines of an office, what he had just witnessed, was anything but.

James had had his suspicions, but the question confirmed them. Ames was reliving recent events and struggling to justify his actions.

James recalled his own baptism. It had been on a battlefield somewhere dusty and inhospitable where the philosophy of fight or die was king, utterly different to the tech environment of a corporate jet and simpler to justify. Still, he wasn't about to be analysed.

"For Ollie, it's like ripping off a sticking plaster. Get it done, there's less pain, less to think about. He uses gallows humour as a shield. Me, I think of society as layered, some of those layers need scraping off."

"That's how you do it, justify it, it's not how you deal with it."

James had been here before and could sense Ames struggling with his conscience, the law was a foundation the man had based his entire life upon, rough justice wasn't sitting well. He liked Ames. If he could shift his perception, he would.

"Right now, Stuart. Your mind is playing games. You're thinking about four men who've just been thrown out of a plane and may not survive."

Ames nodded.

"Think then, on this. How did they get there? What did they do that was so bad?"

"Ok. But still."

"You're not thinking Stuart. What do you suppose they imagined the consequences of what they did to be?"

"Jail, at worst, I suppose."

"Stuart." James paused for effect, then delivered the impact statement. "Not the consequences to them, the consequences for the girls."

It was a flat message, said in a way that stripped victim status from the groomers, and transferred it to where it really belonged and was a question more complex than cause and effect. Ames's mind did an about turn, the men's deeds now uppermost, recalling the callous disregard exhibited by the grooming gang. The fact that unchecked, it would, right now, still be happening.

"I see."

James figured that, in time, Ames genuinely would. But he had another favour to grant. Something that over time, would be needed.

"Stuart, me 'n Ollie, we're lucky. We've been through a lot of stuff together, barely survivable shit some of it, stuff you can't describe, but it doesn't stop your head from thinking about it, remembering it, dwelling on it. Left alone, that kind of thinking is destructive, the little details get to you. PTSD, flashbacks, call it what you like, you're just going over stuff that only *your* mind has in it. But we've got each other, we can validate what we did because we were there. And context is crucial. What you smelt, tasted, saw, did. Was that puff of dust or tiny movement a guy with an RPG? Are you or your mates about to become a statistic? The rights and wrongs of taking a life is completely dependable on circumstances. There isn't a courtroom on the planet that will ever understand how fear builds before a contact, sometimes for days, weeks even. They're armed, you're armed, you're shitting yourself, and it becomes a simple choice, be better than them, live through it and worry about the consequences later. For most vets, there's no-one you can tell, especially these days when years after being faced with a split-second battlefield decision, it gets called out as criminal by folk that will never, ever understand the moment. It's said that it's better to be judged by twelve than carried by six, but that's only because just one of those scenario's is survivable. Imagine though, chucking a couple of grenades into a courtroom, let off a mag or two, fire up the survival instinct and watch a judge and jury's perception change."

Having attempted to settle Ames's struggle with morality, James continued in another, more human vein.

"But the bigger issues, the deeply personal ones need a different treatment so, me 'n Ollie, when one of us needs it, just turns up with a bottle of scotch and two glasses. The first few tumblers are generally sunk in silence, but after a while, the mind, the tongue relaxes, and we remember, and remembering takes us back and we remember the why, not ifs, or but's. As for today, tell me what we just did was wrong. Look at the damage they did in the name of their own gratification. Deeply immoral, evil, yet society would have let them out to crack on and do it again. Their victims don't get that choice. There are no nuances or excuses for what they did and would have continued to do. And they had a shot at surviving. No-ones been killed here, if anyone's died, then it seems to me they reaped what they sowed."

"Why are you telling me all this?"

James smiled. "Because if you ever need to talk, find a nice bottle of scotch and three glasses. We'll know."

Rethink

Nine hours later, they landed back at the estate. It had taken longer to refuel on the homeward leg but as their transit visa now had the correct number of passengers listed, they didn't sweat it. It had been bright and warm in Larnaca, so they'd stretched their legs on the tarmac, glad of the sun on their skin. Leaving Wes and Juddy to sort the aircraft, they made their way to the Ops room, their fresh information paramount, Sacha, Tom, and Bailey were waiting.

The boys regaled the group with a recounting of their deportation mission. No-one demurred, whatever the future held for Faz and his boys, well, they'd deserved it. There was a real sense that their country was cleaner. They knew they'd only scratched the surface, but something was better than nothing.

In the debrief, where all got to voice an opinion regarding their latest tasking, the chat moved on swiftly from past events.

The new intel was troubling as it was obvious that they had a new and immediate problem; attempting to retrieve the missing girls. Not knowing how long they had before the girls were split up and moved on was the crux of the issue. There would be no time for a full reconnaissance. Not ideal. That said, it was essential they got boots on the ground, in itself, relatively risk free. It was a popular tourist destination so their presence wouldn't be striking, nevertheless, it was foreign territory.

The boys went to pack, the others put on standby. Sacha had an immediate problem, non-operational, but an important one none the less. She voiced it.

"I hear you." Said Ames. Then continued, "So what are you thinking?"

"We think she should come home, with us."

Sacha drew herself up, expecting some resistance. "She has no home life. No chance of an education. No guidance, no help, and she's been badly abused. We should help."

"How?" Asked Ames.

"Us. We can do it." Tom surprised even himself, the words having come from his mouth.

Opsec on his mind, James intervened. "She's sharp enough to realise we're not what we seem."

"That girl's been keeping secrets for years," Tom said. "And under the worst kind of pressure. I think she'll understand the value of ours. And anyway, just how much does she need to know? All she's seen so far, is a grooming gang being broken up. There were no guns, just concerned citizens acting in her interest."

"Ok." Said Sacha, determined to get to the nub. "Who thinks we should send her back? After all she did? After all she's been through. Anyone?"

There was a mental shuffling of feet.

"That's what I thought." Then, softening her tone. "Guys, this is what we're here for. Whatever we do, whatever we get involved in, there's always going to be something we couldn't foresee. Lyla is one of those things."

"I'll help." This came from an unexpected quarter. The room turned to face the speaker.

"What?" Said Bailey, seeing the surprise writ large in the group's expressions. "I'm not a machine. I care too, you know."

In the brief silence that followed, Sacha looked carefully at the analyst. Baileys game face had dropped and had been replaced by a disappointed aspect that stirred compassion. This wasn't the hard-nosed, dispassionate Bailey she was used to. She looked hurt. Her tone reflected that as she continued.

"I heard what went on, she coped well. I might get to like her. And she's alone."

"Not anymore." said Sacha, accepting Bailey's stance. A silent accord took place between the two women and the analyst relaxed; her point made. The room settled back into discussing mode.

"So, what do we tell her?" This from Ames, who seemed to have accepted the status quo. "Not the truth, I hope."

"Some of it. But you're right. Not all. She's gonna get a helluva shock when she sees her new pad."

It was decided then, that for the time being, Tom and Sacha would take Lyla to their home and pending recall, stay there. If circumstances required it, Lyla would come back to the estate where Bailey would step in until they returned. Sacha left, smiling, and mentally compiling a shopping list.

Respite

The boys were already there so Tom and Sacha reckoned they had, at best, a couple of days before possibly having to leave for Turkey. It was good to be home. They'd explained Lyla's presence to Inga and Donna with, "She's Tom's niece. She could be here a while."

Needing to stretch out from the drive Tom had headed straight for the gardens, his sanctuary. Lyla was off exploring with Sid, so Sacha visited the girls in the kennels. Tom met up with her back at the main house. He seemed peeved.

"You've seen what she's done?"

"Who?" Sacha asked, innocently. Fully aware of the source of Tom's angst.

"Inga, the madwoman."

"Do tell." She mocked, in her best English accent.

"That little copse behind the kennels. It's a fucking graveyard."

"I think you'll find it's actually a cemetery."

"There's a difference?"

"Yep." She replied smugly. Inga had outlined her idea and had known the distinction between the two.

"A cemetery is a burial ground whereas a graveyard is a burial ground in a churchyard."

"Whatever. You've seen what she's up to?"

"Kinda funky. I reckon."

"I'm having none of that Halloween shit. Crazy women in diaphanous robes dancing around burning hazel twigs 'n surrounded by Indian spirit guides."

"My, my, Tom Hood. What an imagination you have. All she's doing, is respecting the lives of the ones we couldn't save."

"With eye of newt and wing of bat?"

"Get over it, Tom. It's time for Lyla's induction. I'll see you later."

Lyla had taken the full tour, courtesy of the nice, old Australian guy, Sid. It was as plain as the nose on your face that these were not 'normal' people. She looked up from her new iPad, having just linked it to the house internet.

She had no intention of using social media. In the first place, she'd been advised not to, her personal security the foremost consideration, and secondly, she'd never been a slave to it. Her subjugation to the gang not something that could be 'shared', even if she'd had 'friends' online, which she hadn't. She was downloading music when Sacha joined her, on the grass.

"You're millionaires?"

"Yup."

"Fook off."

"Potty mouth."

"Sorry."

"You'll need to write your dad."

Sacha was talking differently now, sounded different. She looked different too. Apparently, her hair had been a wig.

"'ang on. You're American?"

"Yup."

"Foo…" A pause. "Ok. But he won't read it. I'll phone."

"What are you going to say?"

"Pfff" Lyla scoffed. "Not the truth…I'll tell him I've run away, that I've gone to London. He won't give a shit."

Sacha frowned.

"Sorry. It's not easy you know, all this," Lyla offered, looking around. "Changing."

"I know, honey. Let's just see how we go. But we can't have your name appearing on a missing person's list. Tom 'n me will get dressed up, go see him and tell him you've gone into care."

Lyla instantly felt insecure, desperate for someone to care. "You're not gonna dump me? Are you?"

Sacha took Lyla's hands in hers. "That's not what we do, honey. You know that."

Lyla thought back to the first time they'd met. In that poxy, shitty school. They'd promised then to be there for her, and they were. Lyla knew now that they were not official, just people who helped people. That there were more of them, not just Sacha and Tom. There were all those people at the big house; The Palace, as she thought of it, Dave, Neil, Bailey, and some others whose names she didn't know.

"Who's that little girl on the walls? The pictures?"

Sacha spent an hour telling her all about Ellen and what had happened to her, including that The Twins were now dead, and that their death had been an accident.

"Sounds like they deserved it."

Sacha nodded. "That they did, honey."

"Do you miss her?" Lyla knew it was a stupid question but wasn't equipped to ask anything else.

"Every day."

They sat together on the grass, each wrapped in their own thoughts but seemingly content with the company.

Sacha broke the silence. "Tom and I need to go away for a little while."

Seeing the girl's panic, Sacha quickly continued.

"Don't worry, you'll be fine. You remember Bailey?"

Lyla nodded.

"Well, while we're away, you'll go back to the estate, and she'll take care of you. We won't be gone for long and when we get back, this place will be home. If you want it to be."

"Why do you have to go?"

"Honey," Sacha looked Lyla in the eye. "It's about the other girls. We need to go get them."

Lyla, though wary of losing all she could see, tried to understand.

"We can't just leave them." Sacha insisted.

"No. I know." Lyla conceded. "But you're coming back? Right?"

"You can count on it."

Lyla had her promise.

"Can we go see the dogs now?"

"Not just dogs, honey." Sacha brightened. "There's at least one deer, a badger. We might even have an owl!"

Sacha was still reeling the animals off as they went out into the grounds towards the kennels.

It was a lot to take in. They'd spoken to her about how they'd like to help. No strings, no pressure. *'It's up to you.'* They'd said. They'd been waved off from 'The Palace' and come here.

They had a lovely house; it even had a swimming pool. It was clean, warm and her room was like all the best stuff she'd ever seen on the telly. There was masses of space. 'Grounds' they called it. She still wasn't sure how she'd ended up here and right now, didn't care, as long as she got to stay. Sacha and Tom were nice, but more than that, they'd saved her, given her firm ground on which to find her feet. For the first time in her life, she felt cared for. That life, her old life was as shitty as it could get and she had been resigned to the fact it wasn't ever going to get any better; most likely worse, until that day at school, when everything changed.

Sacha had told her that the first step in her new life would be to improve on her education, it was non-negotiable and meant going back to school, except it wasn't really school. She had her own teacher. Yvette, her name was. She would be teaching her here, at the house, no uniforms, no crap food, no pointless assemblies. Just the stuff she'd really wanted to learn but at the time didn't see the point in, and she was also going to learn French. From time to time, she'd be taken to The Palace and its Science Lab and IT suite.

"Can I be a vet?"

"You can be anything you like, honey. If you don't mind hard work."

Pooh and the old house dogs were lovely and every day there was a breakfast in that massive kitchen. The mad birds who looked after the animals were funny, and kind. If she had one regret, it was that there was no-one to show all this to.

Start Walking

He'd lost a shoe and knew from experience that a foot accustomed to being shod, on this broken ground, would very soon tear up badly leaving him unable to walk. And walking would be his salvation. He took off his shirt and vest, ripping the latter into strips to bind his bare foot. He put his shirt back on, noticing the numerous scrapes and grazes that up until now, he'd only been dimly aware of. He was in severe pain from his balls. A deep, visceral ache that wouldn't go away and forced him into a stooped walk. The kicks he'd had to take were very fresh in his memory; it was that memory that kept him trudging painfully south, as they'd advised. South, towards revenge and the parachute he'd seen come down, on an agonising slog towards where he'd last seen it.

If the drop to earth hadn't killed him, Mo might survive, though Faz had strong doubts about that. Eric, he was certain, would not. Faz had seen the ground rushing towards him and even though he'd steeled himself for the hit, he'd landed hard. Eric, drugged, would have piled in. Faz was in no doubt he'd have broken both legs, probably his back. Paralysed, he'd just have to lie where he fell. His pale, freckled, white skin would redden, then burn. He'd be fortunate if thirst and madness finished him off before animals got to him. Either way, his flesh would be consumed, food for the wildlife, his bones picked over, then scattered by animals and the wind. Faz didn't care.

Them, the white boys that had fucked up his life, that was what he cared about. Faz had been forced to give up his bolthole in Turkey. As he'd talked, they'd checked its location and description he gave on google earth, there was no way he could lie and worried at length what he'd find when he eventually made it there, and Faz would make it. If it was the last thing he ever did, he'd make it.

He knew the girls would be gone, that seemed to be their only goal. Beneath the sun and through his pain, Allah spoke to him, kept him moving. His mind wandered, seeking out the crevices where the Quran lingered. Thirsty, hungry; Faz couldn't remember his last meal, not what it was, when it was, or where it was. But he remembered those kicks in the balls, every excruciating step a reminder of his humiliation, his degradation.

From a grim recess came a teaching, Qisas, the law of retaliation, lex talionis, an eye for an eye. And if in the course of following Sharia law, he exceeded the punishment that fit the crime, surely that also is the prophet's will. For an hour he hobbled tortuously onward, then saw a fallen parachute flapping, snagged on a thorn bush.

Tangled and without a knife, Badboy had given up. The tough lines that had suspended him now imprisoned his arms, nor could he see beyond the suffocating fabric that imprisoned him and, in the heat, breathing was difficult.

His landing had been hard, the ground coming to meet him, baked, savage, and boulder strewn. He was convinced he'd broken at least one ankle and the thought terrified him. He was going to be robbed, raped, murdered where he lay injured and helpless. He heard muffled grunting and the sound of approaching feet and whimpered, for some reason, in that instant, he recalled one of them mentioning Kipling, had he known what that meant then the last verse would have terrified him even further.

When you're wounded and left on Afghanistan's plains,
And the women come out to cut up what remains,
Jest roll to your rifle and blow out your brains
An' go to your Gawd like a soldier.

The canopy that enveloped him, moved, something tugging, pulling, he prayed it was human. Despite himself, Badboy first tried playing dead, then, screwed his eyes shut, he didn't want to see what was coming all the while knowing there was nothing he could do to stop it.

Badboy almost wept with relief. It was Faz. But not the Faz he knew. This one wore a ragged, exhausted, desperate expression.

Begrimed, sweaty, the dust turning to black in the creases of his face but eyes bright, feverish almost, the skin around them swollen and purpling. Badboy's sense of deliverance was palpable, his life was saved. Faz toiled wordlessly untangling the parachute, unclipping Badboy from the harness and finally releasing him from the silken prison.

"My ankle's broke, Faz."

"Try standing on it, you fool, before judging." Faz said croakily, his voice box still not quite functioning.

He questioned his motives for seeking out Badawi. There was a limit to family loyalty, a frontier he'd already crossed once in the aircraft when bargaining for what he'd believed to be the last parachute. That the boy had been clipped into another was further proof of the white man's perfidy, evidence of his own betrayal.

The youth had been useful only for his appearance, picking up the girls and readying them, so had been tolerated, his effete posturing and mangling of words an annoying necessity. But that was in the civilised world. Out here, in the wilderness, his western ways served no practical purpose. If the ankle was indeed shattered, Faz would leave him here, a broken Badboy no use to him.

He waited as the youth rose awkwardly to his good foot. Then gingerly tried applying weight to the other. A few attempts, each applying more weight to his ankle, saw a grin crease Badboy's face.

"Hey! Not broke, bruv. Hurts though."

"You will get used to it, or you will die here." Faz said flatly, in a voice devoid of emotion.

"No, bruv. Someone'll find us. Come lookin' for us."

"Badawi, we are not going to be found and if someone comes for us. I think we may not live to regret it. No one is looking for us. We have disappeared. Think, you fool. Look around you. Where do you think we are? Remember how we got here." Faz had had time to acclimatise.

Badboy remembered it all too well; the terror of being kicked out of the plane into an unknown alien world, filled with rushing air and the howl of a receding jet engine. Then relative peace as the parachute opened. Forget Pepsi Max, that was a ride he'd never take again. Surreal man. Then it hit him. Not surreal, real. Way outside his ken, his comfort zone, his centrally heated, petrol powered, cash driven environment. Badboy also recalled the way his uncle had abandoned him and was wary of the bigger man.

"So wadda we do?"

Faz looked down at his shoeless, wrapped foot. Hefted it, then set it forward. Badawi could follow or he could not. It mattered little. He looked south, towards Pakistan. He had money there, family, options.

"We walk."

Reconnaissance

They'd flown in as tourists, Ollie bitching about the howling baby in the row behind.

"We've got a jet, Jimbob, for fuck's sake."

James ignored his friend. Flying zoo class was luxury compared to some of their past modes of transportation but was ammunition to Ollie's wry observations. Ollie took joy where he could find it.

They always flew hand baggage only. Hold luggage could get lost. They never needed much and what they didn't have, they could buy. They carried nothing that would compromise them at airport security, the single pair of combined binoculars and digital camera the only remarkable item. *'Bird watchers,'* he'd said. Image stabilizing with a x10 magnification, they'd do for their immediate task.

Though they knew the location of the villa, they had no idea what surprises might be waiting for them. They'd do an area recce first, then decide what kit they may or may not need.

They'd already dialled up for Neil and Dave to follow and had received confirmation from Bailey that their arrival was imminent. They'd need transport, Neil's forte, and Dave had a local contact for hardware in the event it was called for. James hoped that firepower wouldn't be needed, preferring to use muscle only when on foreign soil. He'd briefly seen the inside of a jail in El Paso and had no desire to repeat the experience, not here in Turkey or anywhere else for that matter.

They believed the four girls were at the villa but had to proceed on the assumption that there may be more. Getting them out of the country was for Bailey, Neil, and Dave to figure out. They passed easily through immigration, Bailey's passport provision impeccable, as expected.

Their hire car and hotel were pre booked as a tourist might, they checked in, found a pair of loungers by the pool, and ordered beer. Ollie removed his shirt, to soak up some sun. James, his shoulder stiff and bandaged from the knife wound, elected not to excite attention, so kept his on, but open. They relaxed and chatted quietly, savouring the chilled beer, then dozed in the sun. The villa was some 8 miles away, distant, remote, nestled in the hills surrounding the resort and it could be a late night. They'd wait for the sun to drop before taking a drive.

In the rear-view mirror, the lights of the resort dimmed to pinpoints then disappeared behind a rise. The highway swiftly losing its sophistication, morphing from smooth tarmac to potholed neglect, its margins fringed by gravel rather than kerbstones. Either side of the road was a dry, craggy, no-man's land, the car's air conditioning detaching them from its austerity. Habitation was infrequent and irregular, the terrain was undeveloped, hilly, and broken. Perfect for their purpose.

They selected a vantage point, to the west and above their objective; the setting sun on their backs, in a convenient piece of dead ground from behind which to observe. It gave them a direct if distant view of the target. Leaving the chilled comfort of the car, they sweated just lying there, simmering as the solar baked countryside released the day's energy beneath them.

The villa was well lit, handy given that their bino's had no light enhancing feature. A useful moon shone overhead, adding tone and perspective so they shot photos while the light was adequate. There was no sign of the girls; though they hadn't expected any, it would have been a useful confirmation. That said, there were only men present. This wasn't a family friendly property, which begged the question, what was it? They hoped they'd find the answer in the under build seen on the plans Bailey had produced.

The property's external security consisted of a substantial, well-lit fence. They knew the accommodation was made up of six bedrooms, three bathrooms, a lounge, kitchen and large outside area with pool and barbecue set in a single storey, white stucco modern villa. Beneath the main structure was a garage cum storage area buried into the hillside with access through double garage rollover doors or from an internal staircase. The footprint including the gardens and up to the fence was around 800 sq. m.

"Take a look through these." James handed Ollie the binoculars.

Three men lounged around the pool, smoking, drinking, taking the occasional swim. They labelled them 'keepers', guessing that to be their role. Cars came and went, their occupants solely male. Some stayed longer than others, though the visitors rarely appeared poolside, finding something else of interest inside the building. This confirmed the presence of at least some diversion within. Mentally and verbally, James and Ollie glossed over that fact, not wanting to imagine what that diversion might be, though both were certain it had to be girls.

As the night closed in, the pool was illuminated in an inviting cool, pastel turquoise. Lying there sweating and dusty, the boys could only itch, dream and wait. Sometime around midnight, the lights of a vehicle could be seen twisting and climbing to the villa.

"Bugger."

"What?" asked Ollie, wishing they'd brought 2 sets of bino's.

"Take a look at that paintwork."

Magnified, it became clear what it was about the picture that had troubled James. A blue and white liveried car with 'Polis' emblazoned on the flanks, a massive light bar completing their dilemma.

"That puts the tin hat on it."

"Let's wait and see," replied James.

There was an unnerving familiarity in the way the patrol car swept onto the property. James watched as a bulky, moustachioed man heaved himself from the driver's seat and entered the villa, reappearing poolside moments later. His arrival was greeted with backslapping and the production of a bottle. Clearly a welcome visitor.

"That's not good." Muttered Ollie.

Bailey's advice before leaving had been, 'trust no-one'. Corruption in Turkey was, with few exceptions and from top to bottom, carried out on an industrial scale. That advice was clearly sound. With a bottle in hand and gun on hip, the policeman made a gesture, clearly a command of some sort as one of the keepers abruptly left his lounger and entered the villa. Minutes later, he emerged, a hand firmly gripping the upper arm of a young, skinny, bikini clad girl. She wasn't Turkish.

James and Ollie looked wordlessly at each other. They had their confirmation. Their attention returned to the pool tableau.

The girl had been stripped and was unenthusiastically swaying to the rhythm of a beat, feeble at this distance, then, the music faded out, and she was beckoned over. In what was clearly a well-versed ritual, she knelt in front of the visitor. He still clutched his bottle, but his gun was no longer on his hip; out of its holster, it was pressed against her pale temple. There was an instinctive movement at James's side, and he held out a restraining arm.

"Nothing we can do." He said flatly.

They were spared the details of her actions, her long, fair hair cascading over the man's loins hiding the minutiae of the act. They saw him arch, then slump, apparently satiated. She wobbled indifferently to her feet, and he waved her away with a careless gesture. It seemed at first that there was a tacit, dull response from the girl and then, even from this distance, the boys saw her stiffen, straighten, then lean down towards the man, a motion of her hand bringing his face closer to hers. Her head twitched back, then sharply forwards as in a mad gesture of defiance, she spat his seed straight into his face.

She appeared unconcerned, almost nonchalant by her act of rebellion and while he lay there spluttering, trying to clear the sticky mess from his eyes, she stood upright, turned, and began a slow, dignified walk back towards the villa. As she stooped to pick up her discarded bikini, the keepers astonished immobility evaporated, and they scrambled quickly from their loungers. They saw the flash a second before the vicious bark of a single shot rang out.

"Fuck!"

In the sure knowledge that it was too late to be of any practical use, the boys buried every instinct and stayed on mission.

The policeman was standing, belt and trousers still undone, arm outstretched, smoking gun in hand. The girl lay nude, face down by the side of the pool, utterly still, outstretched fingers still clutching her retrieved swimwear. A large, spreading stain, black in the artificial light, flowed freely across the marbled tiles. The enraged policeman loomed over her before pumping three more rounds into her lifeless body. She twitched at each; already dead but lifeless inertia overcome by the supersonic hits.

"Are you getting this?"

Ollie knew James was but had to express his disbelief. One of the keepers went to an outside utility and hastily extracted a hosepipe. It soon became apparent that his sense of urgency was only to ensure that no blood stained the pristine pool water. He stood between the pool and the girl and directed the jet to divert her blood to a drain set in the tiles.

The policeman had washed his face using water from the hose and was rearranging his clothing, flicking at the uniform, adjusting his gun belt before settling back in his lounger.

There was a relaxed air about the quartet, as if this was nothing unusual. It soon became apparent that it wasn't. A large, black, heavy duty rubble sack was produced, and the redundant girl stuffed into it. From somewhere, a shovel materialised and two of the keepers strolled downhill with their respective loads to a gate in the fence. A few metres outside, a grave was dug. Ollie looked closely at the surrounding area.

"There's more than one grave there, mate."

It was James's turn to curse their lack of foresight.

"Pass me the bino's." Scanning the area where the men were digging, he saw the cause of Ollie's bleak observation. Here and there, were faint signs that the earth had been disturbed. He counted at least five.

"I think it's time we invoked our rights under the 2nd amendment."

"Oh, yes." Replied Ollie, "But they started it."

Mentally, and with a sense of deep resolve, he added guns to their list of requirements.

They stayed watching until all the lights went out, grateful they'd thought to bring bottled water. There was nothing to say about the dead girl, they thought about it, but didn't dwell on it. That would come later.

It was near dawn that the site fell totally quiet, the policeman having left, handshakes all round. They watched as one of the keepers made a final check of the grounds, triggering motion sensors on the fence lighting.

They took a final quiet drive past the front of the property noting gratefully that in common with every dwelling in this part of the world, the power box was set on an outside wall, adjacent to the road. On arrival back at their hotel, James phoned Bailey, then joined the newly arrived Dave and Neil at breakfast, Ollie was already at the buffet. The boys ate, quietly briefed their companions, then went to bed. The next few days were going to be busy.

Separation

Sacha closed down the summons with her thumb.

"We're up."

Tom nodded; he'd expected the call and was already packed. "You've spoken to Lyla?"

"Uh huh. You ready?"

Tom hefted his overnight bag. "All done."

In the car the mood was gently upbeat; Lyla seemingly content to go back to 'The Palace'.

"It's only for a couple of days, honey. Then, when we get back, we'll get you set up properly."

"Ok."

But on arrival, the news wasn't all good. Bailey pulled Sacha to one side and spoke quietly.

"You're going ahead, just you, I'll join you in a few days."

Sacha realised the implications of this instantly.

"But what about Tom, Lyla?"

"I know," Bailey replied, her tone regretful. "But there's no choice. All the other guys are in country, and we're needed to escort the girls back."

"How so?"

Bailey quickly filled Sacha in on the events of the previous night, then to cloak the barbarity of it, swiftly continued.

"In the absence of any other intel, we have to assume there are at least 4 girls there but there could be more. It's clear now that this is some kind of private brothel, and we know that trafficking has been taking place for some considerable time. We're not even certain if they're 'our' girls yet but we need to get ahead of the game. Whoever they are, they need to be extracted and if they're ours, prioritise getting them home. We can't just smuggle them out; they can't be relied on to behave as we need them to. Some of those girls may have been in that villa for far too long. And let's not forget that for all of them, they were in the hands of the gang before that."

"So, what's the plan?"

"For appearances sake, the girls are going to need female escorts, so Tom stays, and we buddy up instead. Lyla knows him, the alternative is to leave her with PC and his people skills don't stretch to handling a young, traumatised girl; he wouldn't have a clue how to talk to her, and what the hell would she make of him?"

Sacha took this in. Tom would not be happy. Not because he was to be remaining here but because Sacha would be out there without him, and probably in harm's way.

"There's going to be a bit of back and forth. I can't produce the girls' documents, passports, and stuff without the kit I have here. I can get their photos done remotely but they need cleaning up, and not just cosmetically. I've rented a place west of where we think the girls are, it's big, remote, and out of sight. That's where you're going today, it needs setting up for when the boys arrive with their cargo, assuming a successful extraction. You need to get those kids in the right frame of mind to travel inconspicuously. As soon as I've sorted their docs, I'll join you. We'll be the teachers in charge of the trip, as good as the boys are, two guys escorting a bunch of young girls on a school trip will raise eyebrows, we can't have that."

Sacha saw the logic. "Are you going to tell him, or shall I?"

Bailey raised a doubtful eyebrow. "You think it'll sound better coming from me?" Then got the joke. "I'll leave it to you."

As casually as she could muster, Sacha strolled over to where Tom waited, bag in hand.

"Really? Honestly? You're kidding, right? What on earth am I going to do with her?"

"Man up, Tom Hood. You'll think of something."

Tom knew better than to question Sacha's abilities. His instinct would always be to protect her but as she'd pointed out, the boys would be there, and this wasn't a job he could do. He reluctantly began to focus on what to do with Lyla.

"Weapons training?"

Sacha frowned and pointed a manicured finger up close and personal with his nose.

"You'll burn in hell, Tom Hood. No. Not weapons training. You're a bright guy, think of something else. Teach her useful stuff. There's a science lab here, and Adey. There's the IT suite, go running, swimming, teach her to cook, something, anything but weapons training, but right now I have to go."

They hugged briefly then parted, Tom watching Sacha as she strolled away. His mind turned to what to do with Lyla, knowing that somehow, he'd have to build a relationship with her. Then, he had a brainwave, and strolled over to the vehicle workshop.

Lyla brightened at the news that at least one of them was staying, even if it was Tom.

Tom was fully aware that he and the girl had yet to fully engage. He'd remained aloof from choice rather than temperament, knowing that Sacha would need to break ground first, in much the same way as that first day, at the school. But if she was to be a fixture, he'd make the most of this opportunity and hope that he'd live through his choice of icebreaker.

Extraction

It was a beautiful, cloudless, and ultra hot day. Energised by the purpose of her trip, Sacha shrugged off her travel fatigue and did an inventory. Bailey's rental had every amenity, plenty of bedrooms and bathrooms and large communal areas with a great recreational arrangement outside. She set up the photography kit Bailey had sent her with then went shopping. She'd had a brief word with James and Ollie who indicated they'd be moving on Faz's villa tonight.

The past couple of days had seen an industrious Neil and Dave fulfilling the boys kit list. The van was a Mercedes Sprinter, large, nondescript, and although it was dented, and dusty, Neil had declared it to be in good mechanical order.

Dave's shopping list had been more complex but ultimately completed with the aid of a local contact and the liberal spreading of cash. The four of them were in James's room, checking kit, cleaning weapons, and packing rucksacks.

James and Ollie had maintained surveillance. The villa's routine remaining spectacularly unchanged. Keepers lounging, male visitors coming and going and the usual last patrol of the grounds in the early hours. Their policeman had not reappeared, though they hoped that tonight, he might. There were going to be no more dead girls.

They went through the images they'd taken, giving Neil and Dave as full a perspective as was possible. Closed comms and NVG's were tested. The boys had specified that the NVG's be thermal, this meant they would work in complete darkness, the images constructed from heat differences, something the infra-red variety couldn't do as they relied on a light source, however meagre.

The fence could not be climbed, too noisy, it would need to be cut, bolt croppers the obvious solution. James, Ollie, and Dave would carry out the initial incursion which would begin with Neil cutting the power on the exposed supply from the street. Once through the outer perimeter, the three of them would deal with the tenants then, check the under build.

They watched and waited as men came and went, firm in their belief that in the waning hours the villa would settle down. It was near 2am before the last guest left. This was signified by the perimeter check they'd seen the night before, then the snapping out of the lights.

They'd observed the three keepers undertake some vigorous drinking poolside during the evening and were content that their task would be simpler as a result. The moonlight was sufficient to not require the NVG's, but they wore them anyway, fully aware that inside the property was when they'd be needed.

Neil signalled that the power was down leaving Dave and the bolt croppers to muscle their way easily and silently through the gate the gravediggers had used. Suppressed pistols in hand, they skirted the pool, noting grimly where the girl had died, then accessed the villa through glass doors which slid easily on runners. Save for the regular, bustling chirp of cicadas, there was absolute silence, the night windless and muggy with reflected ground heat.

It was agreed they would only kill if they had to, and on soft soled feet, they began checking bedrooms. Dave was the first to emerge from one, a thumbs up indicating the unconsciousness and immobilising of a keeper. James found keepers two and three and made them safe.

All bedrooms were checked just in case and were found empty, but rank from sweat and other stale fluids, their use obvious. They found 3 pistols; one for each keeper which they pocketed, but no girls yet. They knew the location of the under-build access door and crept towards it, then down. It was pitch black and the NVG's came into their own.

They looked floorward and watched their feet descend the staircase, the walls shades of blue, the floor a different hue, thermal qualities deciding the tones. They were in a technicolour environment that needed some decrypting, even their own bodies adding colour to the tableau. Warm pipework stood out until, rounding the bottom of the stairway there was a bright cluster of heat.

Their approach was completely silent and aware that their presence, dressed as they were, would cause alarm, put their weapons away, and as planned, flipped up their NVG's, James totally removing his and lifting his balaclava. He switched on his torch and played it over the pity of prisoners. He counted 8. *'Bingo.'*

"Girls." He whispered, not for fear of discovery, but as a gentle mode of rousing what he assumed would be a harrowed gathering. One lifted her head, her arm defending her eyes from the torch beam. James moved it off centre.

"We're here to get you out." He whispered, in what he hoped was a reassuring tone. The last thing they needed was screams piercing the night. Sound carries a long way in darkness.

"Wot?"

Confirmation, English.

"You're being rescued."

The first girls reply had awakened a couple of the others. James rushed to pre-empt panic.

"British Army. Wake your friends. We're getting you out."

He hoped the words would work. In his experience, the words 'British Army' usually did the trick, allaying fear of black clad wraiths suddenly in close proximity.

He heard names being called, saw arms squeezed, people roused then playing the torch over the entire group, saw that they'd understood what he'd said, as hoped.

"Army? Our army?"

"Yes, Miss." He used the title quite deliberately, aware that the formality would confirm his presence as friendly.

"This is how it works. There are three of us here." He shone his torch on Ollie and Dave.

"We're going to cut these locks, but you must come out quietly, quickly, and with no fuss. We're going to switch on two more torches and then open the garage doors over there. There will be a van outside with a man beside the door. Just get in, make yourselves as comfortable as you can, and we'll be away. Can you do that?"

Confused, disoriented and fearful, nods were the mute response.

"Dave, we need the garage door up, and Neil outside." Dave passed the bolt cutters to Ollie, then silently walked away. The clinking of metal, a snap, and the sounds of a ruined lock hitting the concrete floor saw the girls get to their feet, some helping others, the remainder shaky but unaided, they had no possessions, only what they stood in.

Silently, save for the shuffle and slap of bare feet on concrete, they followed Ollie's torchlight away from their prison. James shone his beam on the cell floor, damp and littered with unkempt occupation, it gleamed back unhealthily.

James went out to the van where he was grateful to note the girls were pliant and docile and obediently climbing aboard. There were blankets and they'd brought food and water. For the time being at least, their immediate needs were seen to. He called Sacha and gave her the numbers and ETA.

Sacha was reasonably content she had all that was needed, any special requirements could be sorted ad hoc. There were 8 and, remembering what the boy's had told her about conditions in the cage back in the UK, she had medical kits, hygiene materials and clothing, more than sufficient for that number. She rearranged the villas accommodation so that no girl slept alone and waited for the van she knew was imminent.

When they arrived, and Sacha saw their condition, she hustled them into the bathrooms. It would have to be done in shifts, 8 girls, 3 showers, but they listlessly did as asked. These girls were used to following instructions, to being controlled.

She cast an eye over each, noting lesions, untreated sores and, stark against their prison grey pallor, bruises, mostly about the face and arms; some of their injuries were fresh and would take time to fade. Their old rags she binned, giving the girls free rein with the new clothing she'd bought.

Dave and Neil were nearby, but out of sight, Sacha didn't want any fears surfacing and understood that there would be some spectres amongst the girls when in the presence of men.

The adults had discussed the girl's appearance, their injuries, bruises, and obvious general lack of care, and how it affected their immediate plans. It was a circumstance they should have foreseen but hadn't. What they'd hoped would be a smash, grab, and get out quickly operation would now take significantly longer to allow the girls to recover.

They had no option other than to remain where they were for the time being. Eight battered young girls created a group image that would invite comment and make up wouldn't fix it; the oppressive heat causing sweat which would wash off the disguise.

A quick extract was now out of the question and the scene at Faz's villa was certain to be discovered soon; they had no idea what the reaction to it might be. James and Ollie had elected to keep an eye on events there and had left earlier that morning. She cooked substantial breakfasts, then, when the girls were full, sat them down.

James had told her about his 'British Army' approach, so she carried on with the subterfuge, her tone carrying the weight of a quiet authority.

"OK girls. It's great to see you. We know what a hard time you've had and we're here to set that right. But it's not over yet. We need to get you back to England to be sure you'll be safe. You know how you got here wasn't right, you have no documents which means we can't get you out using the regular channels, so we'll be here for a while to let you recover, and we sort out your passports."

None of these girls had ever possessed an object as exotic as a passport and an appreciative murmur rumbled around the group.

"After what you've been through, I guess a holiday is a good thing right now so that's what we're gonna do. But it's a holiday with a difference. Those men that had you will probably be looking for you so whatever you do, don't try to leave the villa. We're in the middle of nowhere anyway. The gates are locked to keep people out, not to keep you in, this is not a prison, and it's safe as long as you do as we ask. But first, we need to take your photos for those passports. Your recent experiences have left you all looking a bit ragged, but hey, no-one looks great in a passport photo, and you already look a heap better than when you got here last night. In your rooms, there's make up, fake tan and stuff, this is to help you all look a bit healthier for your pictures than you do right now. Please support each other."

Sacha paused, understanding that there was a culture shock issue at play here. She could only imagine what a confused mess of thoughts and ideas were running through these girls' minds. She needed to get them thinking as a unit, not disparate individuals with their own agendas. Repetition and reassurance were what was needed.

"When you're ready, I'll be taking your photos and someone from home will be here in a few days with new passports for you. I need your dress sizes to get you all uniforms, as when we travel, you'll be as a school party. That way, no-one's going to be looking at you too hard as individuals, your passports handled as a group by your teacher, which will be me. Off you go."

The girls dispersed, aimlessly at first until one of the older ones sat in front of a dressing room mirror and began making repairs. Small groups formed, occasional giggles surfaced as they experimented with make-up and began the long trip back to normalcy.

Afghanistan

Faz was sick of Badboy's constant whining. Mostly about water, food, and sore feet. Faz ruminated that the boy was fortunate his shoes were too small to fit his own feet, one wrapped in the rags of what had once been his vest, and which was fraying with every step. They were both fortunate it was summer. Though the nights were cold, there was no snowfall, dressed as they were and weak, that would have been fatal.

The walk to the main Kabul, Islamabad highway had taken four days. Faz had been in pain the entire time, a deep, visceral pain that he knew was internal damage. The bitch's kicks had driven deep. Further up, in his heart and just as painfully, a hatred festered. Sleep, no matter how tired he was, would not come until exhaustion closed down his body. His voice had improved though the bruising around his eyes were a deep, purple mask.

Two days ago, they had met a shepherd. Faz knew this was Taliban country and despite his initial wariness, the sincerity of the man was hard to question and their need great.

On entering the rude hut. he'd had to cuff Badboy to remove his shoes and the shepherd had noted that Faz had only the one. Faz had no Pashto, and his Urdu was rudimentary. Communications were carried out in a variety of ins hallahs and As-salamu alaykum's. The constant tea offerings pressed on his bladder while beside him, Badboy had no understanding of the culture and had constantly to be watched so as not to cause offence. Faz hoped that Shukran would be understood as Thank you.

The shepherd obviously did not receive many visitors and was keen to display his hospitality. There were no cushions, simply a bare, dirt floor and the food, a freshly slaughtered goat and rice, was served in a large, communal bowl. Again, Faz had to cuff Badboy, who'd attempted to eat with both hands rather than just his right, as was traditional. Despite his deep hunger, Faz made sure that some food was left in the bowl, to indicate that the provision was more than adequate. On leaving, the shepherd gave Faz the shoes from his feet.

The meal had sustained them to the main highway, where they hitched rides. This was the only trade route from Kabul to Islamabad with very little in-between. Once asphalt, it had deteriorated into gravel, making their journey south perilous. The terrain was mountainous, with soaring peaks and accompanying rockslides.

This did not deter the buses and trucks from playing chicken, flipped and flattened vehicles littering the valley floors. Cars zoomed at astonishing speeds, far faster than would ever be allowed on a similar road in the West, if there was one. The Afghans darted out along the sharpest of turns, slamming their cars back into their lanes at the first flash of oncoming disaster. Most of the time they made it, but the occasional screech of metal was met with Insha'Allah and a stamp on the accelerator pedal.

From the back of the car, Faz heard squeaks of terror and western curses, Badboy was becoming a liability, having contributed nothing to their trek. Overloaded trucks groaned up steep inclines. Some got stuck, some fell back, when this occurred, other vehicles and their drivers stacked up behind them, growing angry and impatient, prompting insane passing manoeuvres. Crashes were inevitable and accepted. But they had survived and were here.

Islamabad offered camouflage. The intensity of the city giving opportunities for theft. In this way, their tattered western clothes were exchanged for something more in keeping. Inside the pockets of one, Faz discovered coins. Badboy whined that as he'd stolen the clothes that had contained them, they should be spent on food and was cuffed again for his trouble. Faz stamped the streets, looking for a telephone that worked. The little money they had was just sufficient to get his message out. Hungry, tired, footsore and in pain, his hatred sustained him, as he waited for deliverance.

Recovery

In the days that followed, little by little, tentative and unsure at first, the girls ventured from their rooms until eventually, when not in the kitchen, they were generally to be found poolside.

As weeks passed and bruises faded, they gained a little colour from the sun and took on an altogether healthier appearance. James and Ollie reported that while men had been appearing at the villa, none had yet attempted a forced entry.

Bailey had arrived with the girls' new passports and Neil had had a particularly busy time. The old Sprinter was disposed of, and a newer van purchased. He'd applied privacy film to the glass, blacking out all but the windscreen and laid out with seating and sign written up, it looked the part. With an eye to the future, Dave had acquired and broken-down sufficient lightweight Kevlar vests to line the minibuses interior which Neil had fitted and covered with ply. They would easily defy low velocity gunfire, as from a handgun, and offered some protection from high velocity long guns. Inside and out, it looked completely normal.

Bailey had fixed their inbound paperwork. For all intents and purposes, the girls from the Christian school had travelled by minibus 6 weeks ago on a cultural trip. Their return was anticipated by every computer on every relevant immigration database.

For zone control, when the time was right, they planned to travel in a loose convoy, James, and Ollie up front, followed by the minibus with Bailey driving, and with Neil and Dave to the rear.

Bailey briefed them on the route.

"We need to avoid travelling by air, terminals are too intimate, and we don't want to risk bumping into anyone who might know any of the girls, besides which, a group of young girls this size is bound to attract attention. That leaves us with two other feasible less high-profile routes out, both of which involve taking a ferry to Cyprus."

She brought up a map on her laptop.

"Mersin, nice and close, only 20 or so miles south of here but perhaps too close, for reasons already mentioned, also, the ferries from there are notoriously unreliable, last-minute cancellations apparently the norm. We're left then, with Tasucu, further south from here by about 80 miles. Fortunately, it's also far and away our best route out. Two companies operate ferries from there to Kyrenia, Cyprus. If one's cancelled, we get the other, we'll get tickets for both. Either way, they leave at midnight. It's less than a 7 hour crossing so is ideal in every way. Overnight drive from here, midnight ferry from Tasucu, early morning arrival at Kyrenia. Nicely under the radar."

"Why not simply charter a boat?"

"I did think about that, Sacha, but discounted it. I agree that would help keep the girls safe from being detected but is too high profile." Bailey paused before explaining further.

"Arriving on a scheduled route, with the usual traffic will not excite attention, other than what would normally be expected with this number of young girls in tow. Our departure time helps, most people will want to sleep. I've brought something with me that will help keep the girls quiet."

Sacha moved to protest but was forestalled by a raised hand. "I know, I know. I don't like it either, but we aren't familiar with these girls. We have no idea how they'll interact with others. It will only take one of them to go off piste and the whole thing falls apart."

"I'm not going to slip them a mickey." Said Sacha, bridling at the deception. "They'll have to be told and agree."

Bailey understood. These girls had been used, abused, drugged, you name it, they'd undergone it.

"I'm happy to help you with that, if you need me."

Sacha nodded, content that they were the good guys.

"Once we get to Cyprus, Kyrenia to Larnaca Airport is 50 miles or two hours." Bailey continued. "We'll cross the border in Nicosia at the Palace border crossing. The jet will be waiting. Then blighty. Questions?"

The Villa

It was on their last scheduled day in country that their plans were well and truly scuppered. The repercussions to the girls being taken had started with the arrival of their killer policeman in company with what they guessed to be former 'customers'. They'd broken in and found the place empty save for the desiccated bodies of the three trussed up keepers. James and Ollie had reckoned they wouldn't have lasted more than four days without water and had anticipated their passing without caring too much. There would also be no story to tell.

From their vantage point they watched as events unfolded. They'd expected more Polis to arrive but curiously, none did. Instead, the policeman circled the pool area busy on his phone, making numerous, short calls that soon brought forth a result.

Cars familiar to the boys from when the villa had been in use began arriving, groups of agitated men gathering. Then, the policeman took a call which galvanised him. Shouting instructions which clearly meant 'stay here!' He rushed to his car and took off in a plume of dust and gravel. James and Ollie exchanged glances, then sat to wait it out.

Some four hours later, their patience was rewarded. The Polis car returned but this time with two passengers. As they debussed, it could be seen that one was bulky and even from this distance, clearly in pain, the other diminutive. The bigger man began gesturing and shouting, the policeman patently subservient.

"Fuck me. Who'd have thought it?" Ollie handed the binoculars to James who took them and scanned the scene.

"Faz." James said simply.

"And Badboy."

They turned away from the villa and took shelter behind the mound that had been their vantage point. Both looked at each other, clearly surprised at the new arrivals but both considering what it meant. They really hadn't expected any of the four to survive their deportation, that Faz and Badboy had, was food for thought.

"Tough old bastard." Ollie conceded.

James nodded. "Let's get back to it." Rolling over to face the villa, they resumed their surveillance in a disturbed silence.

The boys had hoped that a reluctance to advertise their involvement in the villa's previous use would mean that any visitors would simply shuffle quietly off, counting their losses. Prior to Faz's appearance, their principal concern had been the policeman, just how involved was he? His casual murder, the act aside, disturbed them. He was plainly used to doing as he pleased, which indicated more than simply a client relationship. Whether this would generate a search was unknown, which was why they were here.

No-one at the villa could have any idea where the girls had gone or how. But Faz and Badboy were here now and had recent experiences to relate. They had to assume that official or not, there would now be a search for their group, marked by the presence of eight, European, white girls. The school trip was off.

Having the confirmation they needed there was no further point in surveillance, and they stole quietly away. They'd return tomorrow.

They had no papers, so from Islamabad, his contact had arranged passage by the most inconspicuous route, an uncomfortable 12 day journey smuggled via a container train through Pakistan, Iran and into Turkey. On familiar territory at last, Faz took stock. His villa was not as he remembered. There were no girls and Burak, his policeman, had no news that was good. He knew nothing other than that three men were dead, and the girls had gone. They could quietly bury the corpses, but the girls were another problem altogether. They knew everything that had occurred at the villa and that knowledge might see Burak hang, or at the very least spend the rest of his life in a prison system he knew to be deeply unpleasant, especially so for a corrupt policeman. Burak could not involve his law enforcement colleagues. Turkey's President was making noises about restoring capital punishment, membership of the EU his only obstacle.

Faz had related most, if not all, of what had occurred back in England and while no-one knew how or where Faz's girls had gone, they had agreed that it had all the hallmarks of the pigs that had thrown him from the plane.

Faz was troubled by their organisation, their facilities and efficiency. He could think of no specific reason for being personally targeted though of course their motives were now clear. Everything revolved around the bitches.

The girls then, were the route to knowledge. Badboy had been enlivened by the presence of sheets, food, drink, and the swimming pool. Giving him instructions to sort out new phones and to find out what was happening back home, Faz then ignored him while he went about the business of revenge.

Opening the floor safe, he took out the means. He would leave Burak to carry out a search for the girls who he personally believed were long gone. Meanwhile, he would get back to England and finish what the men in black started. Lyla was the key.

"Brother. Have they left the country yet?" Faz was irritated. Burak, his policeman, was proving to be less of an asset than he'd thought. He was supposed to pass the girls on to the Albanians, making a profit for Faz in the process, not shoot them whenever he felt like it.

"I don't think so."

"So where are they?"

"Brother." Replied Burak, hopeful that the fraternal reference gave him equality, "I don't have as much influence as I would like. I cannot use police resources."

"What can you do?"

"These men," Burak waved an arm at the group clustered around the pool, "They and others have good reason to find these girls and they also know who to look for."

"They will be enough?"

"They must be, and they are believers, like you and me. I will have them on all the roads, for as long as is necessary. They understand the situation perfectly and are motivated."

"They are armed?"

Faz wanted no evidence of these girls or their rescuers to surface. They were to be cleansed before he could even begin to think of rebuilding.

"They are. You have the money? There will be expenses."

Faz looked sideways at the bulky policeman. The aroma of his sweat beginning to creep into his nostrils. After this was over,

Burak would be fertiliser for the hillside. Faz had already made that decision, it was simply now only a matter of timing.

"I believe this is a cost we should share, don't you, Brother? There are things in my garden that will condemn you, don't you think?"

Burak shifted uneasily. He hadn't even bothered to remove the bullets that had killed the girls and he'd used his police sidearm, the ballistic characteristics of which would be on file. He wanted this over and for his old life to resume. The money would have to be spent. His retirement postponed. Faz fired a parting shot.

"And get me a doctor."

Burak shuffled off, sweating, contemplating his future and the temporary need to cast caution aside.

Adapt. Improvise. Overcome.

"Now what?"

James and Ollie had reported back on events at the villa. All agreed that the schoolgirl plan while still alive, was barely breathing and if it was to be resuscitated, it had to be now.

"Escape and evasion." Ollie offered.

"Agreed. But how?"

Bailey answered with the suggestion that had hovered in their minds since hearing the news.

"Well one way or another, we have to get to Cyprus and as much as we'd like to do that by air, we can't do it from here. This piece of Turkey is just too close to conflict zones for a private jet to be swanning around with a dodgy flight plan however well prepared, and finding a private airfield?" She let the question hang.

"Our initial plan is still viable. We have to get to that ferry."

"I don't like the idea." Said James. "Not one little bit. Faz and Badboy turning up has given the opposition something to go on. We need to rethink."

James was aware that going southeast was out. That way was Syria, a country that only a lunatic would consider a safe haven. To the east was Azerbaijan and Georgia, reasonable targets but just too far away to be a realistic goal. That left only two feasible road routes, both vaguely northwest. Cross the Dardanelles strait via the Canakkale bridge or head further up to Istanbul. But either route involved 1000kms plus cross country. Even then they'd have another 400kms to cover before hitting the Greek border. There were far too many variables for comfort.

"What about heading west." Said James, exploring options.

"Get out on the tourist routes via Fethiye or Marmaris. If we time it right, we'll get lost with a thousand other Brits until Stuart can bring the jet in."

"The jet?" Queried Ollie, ever hopeful that some exclusivity was back on the table.

"It's a busy air lane needing only a simple flight plan. If we're going out that way, we've no choice. The chances of a bunch this big getting seats on charter flights this far into the season is nil. And we really do not want these girls engaging with anyone but us."

James weighed up the negatives. "But it's 12 hours by road to Marmaris and that's on the most straightforward route, which we have to assume we can't use. We'll need to factor in 24 hours of travelling. That said, I'll get onto Stuart, see if it's an option."

"It's worse than that." Said Sacha.

"We might need to split these girls into packets of two, three at the most. There's only Bailey and me to act as 'Moms'. And these girls' heads still aren't straight. They look a heap better than they did, but we still need to get some more sun on their skin, and meat on their bones. They just don't look like tourists."

"We could go full designer on them." Offered Bailey.

"Big sunglasses, expensive clothes, hide them in plain sight. But if we did have to separate, we need to build more trust with them. I think we'll need Lyla for that. Some of them must know her."

This jolted Sacha, the thought of her new charge being brought into their situation discomfiting. Her reservations aside, the idea that Tom would also be here, softened the blow. But there was a risk.

"Has anyone thought that bringing Lyla here is just sticking her head in the lion's mouth?"

"How so?" Queried James.

"Well up to now," replied Sacha, "we've only considered how tricky it is getting girls out without being seen. What if Lyla gets recognised coming in?"

"There's just Faz and Badboy to worry about as far as that's concerned and they show no keenness to leave the villa but if it makes you feel better, we'll bring them in from Marmaris. As you know it's miles from here and chances are that they'll get in without being clocked." said James.

"Me 'n Ollie will watch the villa while Lyla and Tom are travelling."

"Ok." Conceded Sacha. "I'll call Tom."

"All our passports are still good," said Bailey, thinking as she spoke.

"And we have this place for as long as we need. Time may reduce any search, which we have to assume at some level, is already happening."

"Fair enough." Said James.

"We'll chin it out for a bit longer. Me 'n Ollie will shoot back to Faz's villa. We need to figure out just how concentrated any hunt for us is going to be. From what we've seen," he acknowledged Ollie, "There's no official involvement other than a single policeman and I have a hunch that he doesn't want too much of what's happened to go public."

Marmaris

"Brake!"

The hangar wall was looming large, and the car lacked dual controls. All Tom could do was shout instructions and hope for the best. Of all the options Tom could have taken, IT, the science lab even the joked about weapons training would have been significantly less dangerous than teaching Lyla to drive. They were on the airfield and Lyla was having the time of her life. Given the wide-open space they were practising in, it should not have been possible to hit anything, yet here they were, barrelling across the grass and the hangar was approaching fast.

"Brake!"

The car slid to a halt a few feet short of target and stalled. An exhilarated Lyla tried to restart the engine. It lurched forward, still in gear.

"Clutch!"

"Oh. Ok." As she attempted to master the required pedal sequence, Tom's phone rang. He put out a hand towards the girl, indicating she cease all activity. She slumped back in the driving seat as Tom listened. Shutting down the call, he turned and said, "Do you think you could get us back to the workshop without killing us both?"

Parking the car up, Tom and Lyla headed for the Ops room. He showed her the photographs Bailey had used for the passports.

"Do you know any of these girls?"

Lyla began pointing. "That's Tanya. That's Rebecca and that's Carmen. I've seen some of the others but can't remember their names."

"Would they know you?"

"Yeah. Probably. I think so."

"OK, then. How lucky are you? We're off to Turkey."

Marmaris was hot and heaving. Tourists, street hawkers, traffic. They'd left the jet in Rhodes then taken the ferry. On boarding the Gulfstream, Lyla was at first awestruck, then took it in her stride though full of questions. Being introduced to the actual pilots blew her mind. She tried every seat before settling next to Tom.

"Is this yours?" She'd asked, leaning back in the plush leather. It was her first experience of air travel.

"Nope. Borrowed it."

"How long for?" Her eyes saucers.

"As long as it takes. Ok. So, you know what we're doing? How important it is?"

"Yeah."

These past days, Lyla had gotten used to Tom. She could see that he'd done something with her that no-one else had ever done. He'd been nice and because she knew Sacha, knew he expected none of 'that' in return.

They'd been shopping. Properly this time. The clothes were expensive and fitted her beautifully. She was reminded of that film, 'Pretty Woman.' And she did feel pretty; and different, though some of that was because Tom had said she should dye her hair, 'another level of security' he'd called it.

Tom had said that it was her job to talk to the other girls. To reassure them, to stop them being frightened. She knew how important it would be. Tom had treated her like an adult, saying it might be dangerous and that Lyla was the only one that could understand what she might have to say to see that the other girls understood they were being helped, like she had been. Also, she was keen to see Sacha again, and Bailey, in fact, all of them.

She felt safe, even if Tom had said it might be dangerous. Lyla didn't mind. She was so used to being frightened and alone, being scared but with these people around her was something different. She could do this. She tried to stop asking what she knew were silly questions but there was so much that was new. If she could better understand it, she could accept is as real. And she so much wanted all these new things to be real.

Marmaris, this place was called. It was a beautiful, sunny heaven.

"We've got a full day in the car ahead of us. Get some rest."

"Can I drive?" She asked, more in hope than expectation.

"Wrong side of the road." Replied Tom.

"Though from recent experience, I don't see you having a problem with that." He smiled.

There was a warmth to it she liked. As tired as she was, Lyla wanted to take in all the new sights, sounds and smells that buzzed around her. The motion of the car rocked her to sleep.

Sacha was waiting. The car had barely halted when Lyla threw open her door and rushed out to a hug.

Sacha held her at arm's length. "Well, look at you."

Lyla had an elegance lent by her clothing. Her once drawn face had been relaxed by lack of worry and enhanced by contentment. Lyla basked in the compliment, then remembered why she was here and very much wanting to please Sacha, was determined to do her part. "Where are they?"

Sacha led her inside, then left to catch up with Tom.

Though they'd been advised that Lyla was on her way, it was apparent that initially, she wasn't recognised. One of the older girls moved first.

"Lyla? Is that you?"

"Hey Carmen." Lyla had arrived poolside and had deliberately waited to be identified. Inside and out, she wasn't the girl these others had once known. Her arrival created something of a stir and a heap of questions. She instinctively knew that the best way to get these girls on side was to show how different she was now to before, in that shitty house. They were grouped around loungers and a glass dining table. There was a drift of scented smoke and the unfamiliar waft of a barbecue. They looked relaxed, but not. There was a tension amongst them that set them apart from the adults, a gang mentality almost. Lyla understood that. She got to work.

Of Mice and Men

Ames had reluctantly vetoed taking the jet into Marmaris or Fethiye, it was another one of those little things that interfered with the lives of mice and men; the jet was temporarily grounded in Cyprus having developed a fault that would take time to fix. They didn't feel that their departure from the villa could be left while waiting for it to be made airworthy as they were under a variety of pressures.

James and Ollie's continued surveillance of the other villa had paid dividends, it had been transformed from a makeshift brothel into a hub from which a hunt radiated. A hunt that appeared to be directed by Faz and the policeman. If the search intensified or spread further west, their villa would surely be compromised.

The guys weren't built for babysitting and the girls were getting restless, Bailey and Sacha, fielding the bulk of these duties, could sense a rebellion building. Leaving soon was the best of their worst options. No-one liked it, but the adults were all armed.

'Better to have it and not need it.' Remarked Ollie, 'than need it and not have it.'

This was going to be a desperate run for safety, a race that must be won regardless, confident that the people looking for them had no official mandate. The policeman they'd witnessed commit the murder had upped the ante. His casual disregard for life prompting the enaction of Newton's Third Law; every action has an equal and opposite reaction. It wasn't how they wanted things to be, but it was how it was, and all accepted it as such.

As a necessary precaution, Neil had set up a vehicle exchange en route. While they couldn't alter their current identities, avoiding being tracked would aid their efforts. The girls had several changes of clothes in their rucksacks and if they had to, the group would chop and change appearance, party sizes, and modes of transport. A van leaving the villa, might not be how they'd arrive at their destination.

Once in Tasucu, they'd hop a ferry to Cyprus, wait out the aircrafts repair in relative safety and with luck, that would be the end of their troubles. It would be those 12 hours and the wait for the boat that would define the outcome.

James and Ollie had noted that checkpoints had only been set up on the main roads and were comprised of civilian cars, most of which they identified as belonging to Faz's customers at the villa. There had been no sign of helicopters offering an aerial perspective, nor had they expected any and they hoped their route, skirting towns and built-up areas, would see them through.

The plan was that the boys would be a couple of miles ahead, if any checkpoints were encountered, their locations would be relayed to the rest of the convoy which would then take an alternative road if one was available, or reverse course until one was. In that instance, point man duty would transfer to Dave and Neil until the boys could catch them up. With luck, this would offer the middle vehicle, the minibus, which now included Tom and Lyla, sufficient protection. If there was an unavoidable encounter, they anticipated that shooting their way through might be their only option.

They could not be caught and given what was almost certainly an unofficial hunt by what they'd dubbed 'the paedophile militia', they were reasonably settled with the idea that there might be casualties, one sided, they hoped. The tracking on their phones showed where everyone was at any given time. The school party ruse would only work on arrival in Rhodes, until then, they'd simply have to react to events as and when they occurred.

"We can't go home, Bruv."

"Explain." Answered Faz, brusquely. His groin ached constantly; the doctor's examination having aggravated the area. The pain killers he'd been prescribed having little effect.

Badboy had been busy. Though he'd got a new phone and recovered his old phone number, it was useless without his list of contacts. He had nothing to transfer them from and had been lucky using the Cloud, Facebook, and WhatsApp to retrieve some, though not all them. Getting the phone number of Mo's taxi firm had been simple, a quick search on the net finding the website. He'd spoken to one of the senior drivers and had been given the bad news.

"Mayfield is inside, not even been given bail. He's gobbing off about all of us. Everything. The house is closed, boarded up. There's a Paki copper pullin' everyone in. We're fucked bruv. If we go home, we'll get tugged."

Faz had already dismissed the idea of returning to what he now thought of as his old life. The house had contained secrets and Mayfield had provided protection. Both were presently a liability which could not be altered and would, he was certain, condemn him further as they yielded knowledge.

His floor safe had provided the means to return to England; a Turkish passport, his picture the only accurate element, prepared for a moment such as this. His old life was dead to him now, but he had to get back, just one more time. His hidden cash and bank accounts accessed to fund a new life here. His wife and children were baggage that were no longer his concern. Badboy would have to be disposed of. He knew too much, but not yet. Faz had one more use for him.

"The new kafir bitch, the one we were waiting for before all this happened?"

Badboy thought back. "Abby, her name was. What about her?"

"Do you think she can still be of use?"

"I dunno. How?"

Faz's eyed narrowed when he recalled the kicks he'd taken, the one's that caused him pain still.

"The old bitch, the next one up for transport. What was her name?"

"Lyla." Recalled Badboy. "Why?"

Though reluctant to recite his humiliation in front of this boy, Faz did so, though only to express his desire.

"She did this to me. And there was a woman with her. Use one girl to find the other then, in turn, to find the woman. I want them both and if you do this for me, there is a place here for you."

Faz allowed the implied threat that Badboy would otherwise be abandoned to hang between them.

Badboy had already figured out that there was no way of going back to England but had assumed that one way or another, it would be business as usual, with added sunshine. The tourist hotspots would yield rich pickings and poor policing combined with corrupt officials, a level of protection. All he wanted to do was leave the old crap behind, get himself a nice convertible and cruise.

Faz's tone told him that he'd need to be careful, sort the old man out and then take it from there, one day at a time. There was a risk commensurate with the reward though. Abby was dumb and inexperienced, through her, Lyla shouldn't be too hard to track down but the woman? And if he did manage that, how the fuck was he supposed to get her here? He'd play for time and hope Faz's balls went septic and killed him. Then it would be Badboy's playground.

"I'm on it." He said, emphasising the point by studying his phone and opening an app.

Libby

"Why won't they let us have a phone?"

"It's not safe."

"Still, you'd think they'd let us have a phone."

One of the girls was sulking. Lyla had seen her before, at the house, but didn't really know her. Libby, she'd been told.

"What would you do with it?" Lyla asked. Already knowing the answer.

"I dunno."

"Yes, you do, and it would be the stupidest thing ever. No-one cares about you back home. These people do. You have to listen."

"Why do you trust them so much?"

"Because I can. I can trust them. Everything they said they'd do, they've done it and they don't want nothing from me, or you. They just want to help."

"Well, what happens when we get home?"

"There's a place we can go. It's for people like us. We'll be safe."

Though Lyla knew her future lay somewhere else, now was not the time to say so. Now was a time for everyone to be able to see the same thing. Something different to how their lives had been.

Beccy spoke, her eyes sad. "They killed some girls while we were there. At least, we heard a gun go off, and they didn't come back."

"Well, there you are then. The best thing is for you to get better so we can travel and get away. And you don't need no phone to do that."

Libby didn't like this posh, bossy bitch Lyla one little bit. The minute she'd arrived in her fancy gear she'd been pushing everyone around, telling them how nice these people were, how much their lives were going to change. But Libby wasn't buying it, she wanted her old life back, a life where she knew what was happening and had developed a way of dealing with it. She had no use for empty words and promises, she'd been there before and it always ended the same way, back where she was.

She was indifferent to what most of the others saw as forced sex, quite liking the slaps, and biting that came with it realising that actively encouraging the roughness brought benefits; at least when she'd been at the other villa, there had been the occasional puff of weed, or hit of coke. She'd had nothing for ages and awake or asleep, she had a need.

She had to get away from this lot, needed a source but out here in the sticks and with no phone, she was fucked. She pushed back on the urges and hung on; she had to get hold of a phone. Theirs, the adults, were no good, she couldn't get past the security screen. But she'd noticed that Lyla had one. She'd try tonight. But first, she had to find a way of being her roomie.

"Sacha?"

"Yes, sweetheart?"

"Libby's asking if she can move into my room."

Sacha had spent enough time around these girls to know that Libby was a problem and had discussed it with Bailey.

"They've come along nicely." Sacha had remarked, watching the girls around the pool, smiling, and interacting, a far cry from the disoriented, fearful group that had arrived.

Bailey had nodded thoughtfully, replying, "Have you spotted the weak link?"

Sacha had. Libby, one of the girls held longest, was a staunch complainer. Always wanting more than was available or safe. They'd tried explaining what their situation was and the need for a low profile, but what Libby wanted, she wanted it now, and her vocal complaints were wearing and influential. The group was beginning to splinter into the wants and the want nots. Her principal complaint was the desire for a phone and no number of explanations as to the dangers of this were enough and were met with a sullen glare.

Bailey was grateful all their units were pin protected and therefore of no use to anyone but the owner. Nevertheless, the adults kept a firm hold on the devices, Libby having been caught trying to access one but defeated by the pin code.

"That might be a good idea, honey. She seems to have more problems than the other girls. You spending more time with her might help."

Lyla was reluctant. There was something about Libby that made her feel uncomfortable, itchy, something in her eyes that said she was trouble. Still, if Sacha thought she could help, she'd try.

"Ok. I'll go talk to her, help her move her stuff over."

Libby was all chat and gratitude, a complete change from earlier. Perhaps Sacha had been right, after all.

"Thanks Lyla. Your room is so much nicer."

Lyla knew it wasn't, the bedrooms were mostly the same but as they were new around each other, figured Libby was talking for talking's sake.

"It's ok." She replied. "It's nice to see you feeling better about things. I wasn't sure at first, you know, but Sacha and the rest of them are lovely, really."

Libby didn't care how lovely anyone was or how easily fooled this dumb cow was. She was no better than her or the others, just thought she was with her nice clothes and sunglasses. Libby couldn't wait for bedtime to come.

She'd forced herself to stay awake, the ache in her belly helping. Creeping from her bed, she stole across the room and cracked the blinds open. Moonlight entered the room, but Lyla never stirred.

Freeing the selfish cow's phone from its charger, Libby hesitated, watching, but Lyla was fast asleep. She held the phone up to Lyla's face and hoped that even with her eyes closed, it would know its owner. It brightened in recognition, then showed the home screen.

Back in bed, Libby got beneath the covers and screwing her eyes up in concentration, recalled Badboy's number.

"Bruv!"

Faz heard the shout and looked up. Badboy, dishevelled and bleary eyed from sleep, rushed into the room, a triumphant phone held high.

"I've just had a text!"

"Explain." Said Faz, still thinking of the Albanians.

"One of the girls that was here, that was taken, I woke up and there was a text."

"Saying?"

"She's with them, she's in a villa, somewhere, but deffo still in Turkey. And Lyla's there, with a woman."

Faz immediately shelved plans for travelling back to England. *'They were here.'* The cause of his pain.

"Have you text her back?"

"Not yet. I just got it." Badboy stood, his phone like a live thing in his hand. He'd just illustrated how useful he was and was now waiting to see how Faz would greet his value.

"Sit down, boy." Faz patted the sofa.

This was the first sign of any chinks in the oppositions armour. It must be exploited. Badboy grinned enthusiastically and did as bid. He'd felt his grip on their relationship slipping, particularly during the long trek through the mountains. There had been no tech for him to fall back on, no way of contributing when isolated from the modern world. Now he was back.

"Where is she?"

"She doesn't know, just that they haven't left yet. I've got names, all sorts of good shit."

"Can she be controlled?"

"Bruv," said Badboy, "she contacted me. She's nicked a phone to do it. What do you reckon?"

"Find out where she is."

"No problem."

Badboy had told her to activate find my phone. When she got the message, she'd do as she was told and they'd know exactly where she was, and the rest of them with her.

"Except she can only have the phone out when no-one's around."

"Brother, that is not a problem. We simply have to know where they are or will be. Then they can be dealt with."

Dismissed with a wave of the hand, Badboy went outside to the pool. Taking a lounger, he skinned up and began to compose.

"Sacha, my phone, it's missing."

"Have you lost it?"

"No. It was charging by my bed last night. Someone's taken it. And Libby's not in our room."

"Where is she?"

"Dunno, but one of the toilet doors is locked and there's no answer when I knocked."

The door was solid, unyielding, and as much as they didn't want to induce any panic into the girls, it had to be broken down.

"Dave." Said James, nodding at the door.

Taking a couple of paces back, Dave launched 15 stone of weight and not a little momentum at the door, the frame gave way, the lock splintering. He followed through, seeing Libby frantically typing on the missing mobile. He grabbed it and she fought back, screaming.

Lyla was right behind him. "What have you done, you stupid cow?"

"Fuck you. Fuck all of you!" Libby shot between Dave and Lyla, running down the corridor and into her bedroom.

"Let me look at it." Bailey said, quietly, hand outstretched. Then went into the kitchen, sitting down with the phone open.

"We've got 'em, Bruv!"

Badboy had told Libby to install old faithful, his Find my Phone app. The instant locations had been shared; he'd nailed them. About 40 miles away, still in Turkey.

Running

"We'll be travelling light folks. If you can't run with it, don't pack it." It was a policy that had served Ollie well on more than one occasion. Now that Faz and his mates knew where they were, the villa was busy with last minute preparations to leave it.

In the weeks that had passed since the girls' extraction, they'd healed a little and relaxed a lot, the pool a focal point. This had been a deliberate distraction designed to alter their appearance and up to a point, had succeeded, their skins taking on a gentle glow, a far cry from the jail pallor once endemic throughout the group.

Libby was sedated. The other girls, on hearing that she'd told Badboy where they were, had been close to lynching her and a few blows had been struck. Sedation had been the only choice, taking the tension from the situation. No-one wanted to beat up a sleeping girl. They'd put her on the back seat, out of the way.

"All aboard."

It was Neil, standing beside the open side door of the Mercedes van. Local tv and radio had given no indication of events at Faz's villa, but Ollie and James had maintained light recces of the area and noted vehicle check points, even having to pass through a couple. It was becoming evident that there was no official nationwide hunt for the girls. These checkpoint guys were not police, they bore no insignia and were marked only by the wearing of hi vis tabards, easily purchased anywhere. As two men, James and Ollie had been waved through but noted that vehicles with girls in, however few, were more heavily scrutinised.

As originally planned, they were heading for the Tasucu ferry, or at least, the minibus was. Bailey, on examining the stolen phone, had informed the group that there was now an active app installed that showed where they were. By the same token, it also illustrated where the other, receiving phone was. This had given her an idea, so to the surprise of the group, she had first left the app active then explained her thinking.

"The texts tell us that it's Badboy on the other end. His phones locator tells us that it's at Faz's villa, so far, so good, all stuff we've confirmed with eyes on. Reading through all the texts, Libby told him she could only use the phone on rare occasions and probably not during the day. She didn't get a chance to send anything saying she'd been found out. She appears to have been more interested in drugs and 'rescue' than anything else."

James ran with what he assumed was her train of thought. "So, we can use this to our advantage?"

"Quite." Replied Bailey.

"The idiot on the other end hasn't thought this through. If he can track us, the opposite also applies."

"Keep going." Said James, happy at the thought that some classic disinformation techniques were about to come into play.

"Tom, and Sacha take the minibus with the girls down to the ferry. Please be aware that we can't predict where the opposition are, just whoever is tracking us." She nodded to James, Ollie, Dave, and Neil.

"The rest of us take two cars and this phone. I'll leave you to decide what happens when they eventually track it down."

"I like it." Said Ollie. "I'll just go and clean some guns."

Burak still had been trying to call all his checkpoints in, but one was yet to respond, he put this down to bad practice on their part, either asleep, or drunk. The remainder of his men were here.

"We know where they are and that, later tonight, is where we are going. When we get there, none of them leave alive. Is that understood?"

"Even the girls?" Came a disappointed comment from one of the gang.

"We can get more of them." Interrupted Faz.

"But there are two I want alive." He described Sacha and Lyla as best he could.

"The others you can do want you want with but afterwards, they die. Clear?"

Faz sensed that the rape and kill order had released a small thrill amongst the men. He received a murmur of assent.

"We will leave tonight, take them in darkness."

He took Burak by the arm. "I will travel with you."

The girls convoy departed the villa around midnight. At Eregli, it split. The minibus taking the dual carriageway invisibly west, Bailey, Dave, and Neil going southwest on a narrower, single lane road. James and Ollie remained at the villa. In time, they intended to follow Bailey's car, but were staying at the villa for the moment with Lyla's phone lit up like a beacon and giving the impression that the group had yet to move and at the same time illustrating that Badboy, at least, was still at Faz's villa.

Bailey had said that no amount of calculating speed and distance could predict an arrival time for the minibus at the ferry as they had no idea what they might meet on the road. So, they were going to wing it. Ames was in Cyprus with their way out, getting the girls to him in one piece was the only aim.

They'd been travelling quietly for a few hours before running into trouble. The checkpoint was set up just after a bend and in the front seats, Dave, Neil, and Bailey's car was being flagged down before they had a chance to react, hi vis vests reflecting in their headlights the only warning.

"Looks naughty."

Dave mumbled from the driver's seat, before powering down his window with Neil following suit. The purpose behind their windows being wound down twofold. Firstly, conversation with the checkpoint was impossible without it and secondly, shots fired through glass are easily deflected off target and the subsequent lack of a window and presence of broken chips suspicious in itself.

They were in a reception black spot and were just about to move when they saw the car coming. Burak had warned them that the girls would not be alone, Faz's narration explaining the presence of at least three, white European men. Locals they could ignore, anyone else was to be scrutinised. They decided to pull this last one over, then relocate.

"You are out late."

"Or early." Replied Dave.

"What is your purpose?"

"How's that your business?"

Dave was doing the talking. Neil sat quietly, awaiting developments, Bailey in the rear seat, following suit.

The unshaven Turk was tired, impatient, and irritated. He'd never liked yabanci. Foreigners who came to his country and pleasured themselves at the expense of his culture. This one was typical, arrogant, and sure of himself. The road was dark and seldom travelled this late at night, less so by tourists. And Burak had said that a show of force would not be out of place. He took his pistol from his waistband.

"This is my business." He said, waving the muzzle of the gun in the yabanci's face.

It wasn't the first time Dave had been up close and personal with the barrel of a gun and he noted professionally that the bore was filthy, and the slide showed traces of rust. Nevertheless, it was a gun and even a dirty gun can go off. He kept calm. If he had to, he'd shoot the man through the car's bodywork, but not before he'd deflected his aim.

"Is this a robbery." He allowed his voice to pitch up and his face to show alarm.

Demir hadn't considered this an option before the man had uttered it. Now though, it appealed. Yabanci's always carried money, had good watches and phones, and there might be profit in what had till now, been a chore. Also, the woman, though a little old for his taste, would provide some entertainment.

"Get out of the car. You," he waved the gun at Bailey, "Stay where you are."

He stood back and lowered his gun to waist height but level with the man's face. He knew he looked threatening and manly, he lifted his chin and looked down contemptuously at the man in the car. In his periphery, he watched his compatriot, Aibak, draw his pistol and circle to the passenger's side.

Dave and Neil understood the difference between a risk and a calculated risk. For this reason, their weapons always had a round up the spout and were ready to fire; the sound of a cocking action was unmistakeable and gave warning.

Exiting a vehicle while under the barrel of a gun was a drill they were more than familiar with and something that had been necessary more than once. Doors could be used as shields, weapons, or distractions but speed and synchronicity were the main mechanisms.

As Aibak drew level with Neil's door, on the pretext of moving slowly as ordered, they released their door handles and clicked open the locks. Their would-be assailants were lost in a bewilderingly swift sequence of events as Demir was hit by Dave's door being flung wide open, striking his hand, and sending his pistol clattering. Neil exited simultaneously, his pistol up. Bailey right behind him. Two shots to the chest felled Aibak who went down and didn't move again. Dave burst from the car and dropped a knee on Demir who was scrabbling to retrieve his lost pistol. Grabbing the man's hair, he rammed his head twice into the unyielding tarmac.

"Bandit country." Said Neil, grinning and standing over Aibak, his pistol smoking and steady.

"Shall I?" He asked, ready to administer the coup de grace.

Dave shook his head. "I wish, but no. It doesn't sit right."

Neil strolled to the side of the road, where it edged onto a steep, stony, hillside.

"How about we just chuck him down there, if that doesn't offend your tender side?"

"That works." Dave assented. He knew that silencing the man permanently would have been the best and safest option, but this wasn't war, not as he knew it.

Together, the three of them stripped the would-be bandits of phones and ID. The dead man went over the side first, followed by his limp companion. Their weapons were examined and found to be minging, not even cocked, more a manhood talisman than a useful tool. Dave broke them down in disgust and threw the parts after their former owners. Neil, meanwhile, was policing his spent brass, which he pocketed for disposal further down the road. He'd contemplated digging the killing rounds from the dead man's chest but discounted the idea; too much blood with no means of washing it off. The evidence they left behind might be a problem for Dave, but he doubted it. Dave was a careful man when it came to acquiring weapons, provenance always a consideration. They'd discuss it, over a pint, later.

Gloved now, Bailey got in the Turks car and drove it a few miles to a side road where she left it, keys in the ignition, in the hope it would soon be stolen. After that, there wasn't much else they could do to tidy up and so got back on the road. The T junction was 40kms away. Bailey contacted James and Ollie; the road ahead was clear. It was time for them to leave the villa. They had a few more hours of dark to work with and resolved to make the most of it.

Ambush

"I can't raise Aibak or Demir. I've sent a car to find them."

"What? Neither of them? When did you send out the car?"

"They have been silent, so I sent Kerem and Sarp an hour ago."

The missing car, apparently unaware of his recall, was still operating under his earlier orders. Burak had given strict instructions that everyone must check in hourly. If they had no reception, they should move to a spot where they could communicate. All had phone chargers, the chances of two phones being out of use were practically nil.

"Where was their checkpoint?"

"Near Eregli. On the D330."

"Which D330? Fool. There are 2 near Eregli."

Burak knew that at Eregli, the D330 split into two. The main dual carriageway which continued to Konya and a smaller, single carriageway to Karaman, where it ceased at a T junction which ran north to south.

"To Karaman. They were on the smaller road."

'West then,' thought Burak. And went to wake Faz.

Rumbled from a pain disturbed sleep, Faz rolled gingerly from his bed.

"What is it?"

"We have lost contact with a checkpoint. Something I expect only in the most extreme circumstances. I think the foreigners might have left their base and are heading west by road."

"Where does west go?"

"Anywhere that isn't east or south."

Faz raised an eyebrow in annoyance at the cryptic response. Burak, seeing this, continued. "You are the one with all the answers, your tracking device that has yet to move, and you tell me they are still here. So why can I not raise my men?"

Faz's response was forestalled by a shout from Badboy. "They're moving!"

"Which way?" Burak called back.

Faz came into view, his phone outstretched. "Have a look."

Burak studied the small map, the dot steady but going south.

"I know this road, and they must pass through my checkpoint, also, the car I sent is heading that way. I will keep trying to raise my missing men, but we must move now to catch them."

There was no sign of Aibak, Demir or their car. They had been here before, had manned this checkpoint and knew exactly where it was, or should have been. They got out and in the dawn light, scanned the area.

"Over here!"

Kerem crossed quickly to where an agitated Sarp knelt in the road.

"Blood." Said Sarp, rubbing the tips of his fingers that had investigated the small, scarlet puddle.

"What's that?"

Kerem had heard a voice. Faint, but a voice, nevertheless. It was coming from below the steep embankment as it edged the road. The two men, on exploring the area, saw movement beneath them, some 20 metres downhill. Together, they scrambled down the hillside, disturbing gravel, stones, and dust, until coming across a dirty and bloodied Aibak.

"Yabanci's. Foreigners. Three of them. White men and a woman." Aibak murmured, breathing hard, his forehead a bloody, crusted, drying mess.

Together, and with some cursing and difficulty, they hauled him up the hillside, placed him in the car and turned, heading for home. Kerem got on the phone.

Burak had a problem. Their quarry was on the move, that much was certain, but ahead of the glowing dot there was less certainty. Kerem's call said as much, something had killed one of his men and disabled another. He looked again at the totality of the map. He was now convinced that the Yabanci's and the girls were heading to the T junction at Karaman. Had they been truly headed towards Marmaris, Antalya, or Fethiye they should have taken the wider of the two D330's direct to Konya and continued west from there. Now, the missing checkpoint lit up the alternative.

He had consulted with others and had discovered that the foreigners could turn left at the T junction and head south to Silifke, then take the road west to Tasucu, from where they could either take the ferry service to Cyprus or keep going along the coast road which was dotted with numerous other small ports that ran similar services or where they might even have their own boat already waiting, Faz had warned him that these people were well resourced. He was convinced now though, that they intended to leave by boat, the key was to stop them before Konya in the north, and Silifke in the south. If that failed, the foreigners would likely disappear and in the event that happened, so would Burak.

Setting that decision to one side for now; while there was still a chance of resuming his previous life, he would send a car to Konya then have it search south. Everyone else would follow him to Silifke. His light bar and siren would clear the way.

"Turn left at the 'T' then look for the right spot." Bailey put down her phone. James and Ollie were behind them on the road and leading Badboy's app by the nose. She judged the boys to be about an hour in their wake, plenty of time to get things set up, then, they'd sit tight, waiting for the boys to arrive. Then, James would leave the vehicle and Ollie would keep driving, Lyla's mobile still bleeping away, leading the paedo's straight into a trap. Pretty much on the nose, the boys drew up and James alighted, the car barely halting.

Ollie drove off in a spray of gravel shouting, "Wankers! I miss all the fun!" His next task was to be the fox in the hunt, drawing the Turks on. Then to stop, blocking the road to prevent any innocent involvement.

James was happy with the selected ambush point. It reminded him vaguely of the Italian Job. They were set up just after a bend in the road, with a steep hillside to the right, and a valley dropping off to the left.

'No JCB or tunnel,' he mused, then, strolling over to the car that had brought Bailey and the others here, began whistling to himself. Across the road, in cover where the lip of the valley met the tarmac, Dave could hear the faint strains of *'On Days Like These.'* He settled alongside Bailey, waiting. He watched as the whistler got into the car and drove back the way they'd come, towards their pursuers.

"I think they've stopped bruv!" There was a moment of confirmation. "Yep, deffo, the dot aint movin'."

Faz itched in his seat. He knew they were closing in and prayed to Allah that the women would be amongst them. He would deal with the Lyla bitch first. His balls ached interminably; under Faz's questioning, the doctor had reluctantly conceded that the damage could be permanent. He had yet to test whether this was true. He would make the old bitch watch while he killed the girl slowly, see if his manhood stirred, and if it did, give it to the woman. They were travelling at speed, and he barely noticed the car on the side of the road, its driver with his head under the bonnet.

As the convoy passed, James spoke into his mic.

"Cop car up front, going like the clappers, looks like Faz is in it. Five others strung out behind."

He slammed down the bonnet and gave chase. He was the cork in the bottle.

Burak saw the tight bend ahead and slowed, he was in a hurry, that was true, but not so much that he would get himself killed on these narrow roads. Beside him, Faz was sweating, concentrating, and Burak could sense a bubbling hatred. Badboy in the back seat, his eyes glued to his app, was relaying their proximity to target.

Had it been night-time, the man in the centre of the roadway would surely have been killed. Instinctively, Faz stamped on the brake, wondering briefly if he had really seen a gun in the man's hands. Confirmation came as his right foot was at its furthest downward thrust, the brakes responding too quickly for the car behind. The ensuing rear shunt occurred simultaneously with his windscreen shattering. The hot breath of a bullet passing his ear and taking Badboy serendipitously first through the upheld phone, then in the throat.

Burak was stupefied and reason said that he should accelerate, but all reason had abandoned him as he grabbed at the warm splash of blood spattering the back of his neck, mingling with grime and a sudden outpouring of sweat. He had to get out.

Faz was shouting and swearing beside him. "Keep going, you fool!"

But Burak had had enough, the last few seconds had unmanned him. Unable to see through the splintered screen and fully aware of the valley that lurked for the unwary, he brought the car to a sudden and complete halt and abandoned it, knowing only the terror that was in front of him. As he hastily exited, his fingers slippery on the door handle, he felt the hard and sudden impact of what he knew to be bullets. It was the last thing he understood.

Behind the police car, multiple collisions had occurred. Not least the one James had caused deliberately by using the classic pursuit intervention technique, or PIT, taking the rearmost car on its back corner. Holding his line on contact, he pushed through, sending the car in front into an uncontrollable sideways slide which ended when it left the tarmac and toppled over the edge of the valley, cartwheeling end over end in a confusion of bodywork, separating parts and mangled occupants. Its nosedive was an anticipated but unexpected bonus, less arseholes to take out manually.

Screeching to a halt sideways on, he exited the car and ran, firing as he went, towards the melee of men and knotted vehicles. After firing the first shot, he hoped that as planned, Neil had moved to the rim of the valley, away from the line of fire of the others and a quick glance confirmed this, Neil sideways on, continuing to pour fire into the first car.

Pressed steel bodywork is good for stopping rain, not bullets, and any impacts were going to be followed by abruptly misshapen lumps of lead pinging off in a haphazard trajectory. Aware of this phenomenon, the ambushers were carefully positioned up range; to do any damage to them, stray rounds would literally have to do an about turn but nevertheless, James and Neil, exposed on the roadway, kept low. James watched as his rounds perforated steel panels and glass, then the flailing, panicked occupants, and could see his colleagues defilade gunfire having a similar effect.

From the corner of his eye, he saw Dave and Bailey working as a team. He knew the system. Dave had opened fire first, Bailey waiting patiently until two shots had been fired before joining in. When Dave was out, Bailey was still firing. It was the action of a second or two for Dave to recharge and carry on putting rounds down allowing Bailey in turn to do the same. Continuous munitions going mercilessly downrange, an irresistible barrage of lead.

The police car was ignored for the time being, it was dead and blocking the road. Between James and it was where the danger lay, four cars with numerous occupants, all armed.

Neil had taken on the car that had collided with Burak, swapping his aim from front seat to back. He'd emptied thirteen rounds into it before he was satisfied and then joined Bailey and Dave. James was still firing in enfilade, straight down the axis. Aggression and ammunition was the key, they all knew. Not many men would stick their head above this parapet, but inexperience would keep them in what they believed to be cover from sight, inside their cars. It was a fatal, rookie mistake from which none would recover.

As the sound of gunfire petered off, then stopped, one car slowly disentangled itself from the others and began rolling on its tyres, a dead hand on the steering wheel, then reaching the edge of the road, tipped into the valley, where dust still radiated from James's PIT efforts earlier.

The only body in the road, was that of Burak, taken down early in the exchange when attempting to leave his car. No-one else had had the time or forethought to do the same and had died in their vehicles, which were now dripping blood from punctured panels.

Coming from behind cover, the four moved cautiously forwards, checking occupants. There were no walking wounded. One still breathed but was immobile; Faz, in the front of the police car, his seat belt still in place, too bloody to tell if he'd been hit or spattered, a pistol waving weakly in his right hand.

James came from behind, jamming the still hot muzzle of his pistol into the fleshy temple. There was no response. He pushed the pistol harder into Faz's head, a clear instruction, there was no way he was going to be injured by another fat man, Ollie would never let him hear the last of it. The action prompted Faz's gun hand to go limp. James reached into the car and seized the weapon, opened the door, released the seatbelt, and pulled the man from the car.

Faz was bewildered and terrified by events. On his knees, doubled over in agony, his mind wandered. Life had been good. Then, on the turn of an unfriendly card, all had changed. He'd been beaten, kicked, thrown from an aircraft, forced to tramp in the wilderness when all he'd ever wanted to do was fuck little, white girls. This was not an appropriate response.

He could smell blood, knew some of it was his, the pain in his balls forgotten as something harder tugged from deep within. And where was his government when he needed it? He looked up and saw a tall, white man with a pistol.

It had been a while and James had forgotten to count his rounds. He was reasonably sure he had at least one left but resolved to spend more time on the range, it was an easy fix. He looked down at the stricken figure, raised his pistol and tested his maths. The bullet erased the last of the fat man's thoughts and he jerked spasmodically, then slumped to the road, the life gone from him. James checked his mag. It was as empty as Faz's mind.

James sighed. He wasn't one for regret but at the same time was a realist. He consoled himself with the image of the dead girl poolside, those weeks ago, and not only of her, but others. Victims of men such as these. Men now dead because they simply didn't know how to behave. He tensed briefly as he heard the vicious bark of a single shot. He looked to the side, where Bailey was moving from vehicle to vehicle tidying up. James stiffened, looked fleetingly skyward, then relaxed, as the dead girls image came again.

With an effort, they stuffed Faz and Burak back into the riddled police car. That, along with the others, they trundled over the edge; more wreckage to litter the valley. The authorities could make of it what they would.

Dave assured them that their weapons were untraceable and as all the magazines had been charged with gloved hands, the empty cases would yield no evidence. These they shooed off the road after the cars.

Not a shot had been fired in retaliation and they hoped now that they had a free run to the boat. All that was needed now was to reunite with Ollie on the one hand and the minibus on the other.

On noting the dropped signal from Badboy's shattered phone, Ollie had performed a U turn and was back with them within minutes. The smell of cordite still hung, and he sniffed appreciatively.

"All done?" He asked, with an air of regret.

"Yep. Sorted." Replied James.

James's car was damaged but driveable. To avoid any future comments on its condition, they drove it on for several miles before sanitising it, then fly tipped it into the valley.

With the five of them now in the last remaining car, they had an uncomfortable ride ahead. A phone call established that the minibus was now coming south, towards them. Theirs had been the hoped for uninterrupted journey.

The now reduced convoy reunited, and adults redistributed, the journey to the ferry was uneventful, not even the anticipated official checkpoints interrupting progress. They put some speed on, the smooth tarmac bordering the Mediterranean being covered at pace.

Arriving a little early, they parked up short of the town and Sacha spoke to the girls.

"OK girls, we're nearly there."

She hesitated, hoping the words came out right. They couldn't risk any of these girls mixing with other passengers, they needed them out of it.

"We're all tired and you probably need to sleep. Bailey has some medicine in her bag. It'll help you relax."

At the prompt, Bailey produced a small pill bottle. Sacha knew they were a concoction of Adey's creation and had been assured they were safe, in moderation.

"One each, take it with some water please girls."

They were handed out and taken quietly and without complaint. Libby was checked and further sedation carefully administered. With their cargo settled, the small convoy moved on towards the waiting ferry, the thrum of the van engine and rhythm of the vehicle combined with the effect of the tablets, gently setting the girls slumbering.

Midweek meant that the ship was not as packed as it could have been. Modern and maintained, its decks were filled with cars and a scattering of vans and minibuses, its clean, white superstructure lit up for loading.

They'd arrived early and so were amongst the first to board. Guiding the minibus to the bow of the ferry, and parking as directed, Neil affixed a reflective windscreen sunshade, this, combined with the dark, tinted windows, shut the interior to prying eyes. The van was locked and left.

The deck crew weren't paying any attention to vehicles already set in place, busy with hand signals, packing the cars as closely as possible before moving on. There was a schedule to keep and their task repetitive. No-one noticed that the secured van was still full of sleeping girls.

The tablets had been a necessary evil. Regardless of the fact that it was gone midnight they still felt it unwise to allow the girls the freedom of the ship. Other passengers were sure to be about, some alert, and they still weren't fully confident that none of the others harboured similar ambitions to Libby.

Having checked, Bailey had said that passengers weren't permitted to stay with their vehicles during the crossing and hoped that the darkened windows and shaded screen would hide the fact that the girls still slumbered within.

Adey had guaranteed that anybody taking one would get 12 hours of sleep from the pills he'd provided and reluctant as they were to leave the girls unsupervised, they hoped they'd done enough and walked through into the passengers seating area. They grabbed some food and settled into comfortable, high-backed seats set in rows.

Seven hours later, they docked in Kyrenia, their passage across the Med calm and uneventful. The sun had been up for an hour and the girls were waking as they disembarked and drove though immigration. The checks were cursory, part of the routine of life, just another vehicle passing through the busy port.

There had been some traffic, expected at this hour as Cyprus woke. Some two hours later, they passed easily through the Palace checkpoint in Larnaca and were at last, on friendly territory. Ames was where he said he'd be, parked on the Cypriot side.

"No further problems?" They'd made him aware of the roadblock and as he spoke, he was scanning the minibus bodywork for signs of damage.

"None. Replied James. "Is the jet fixed?"

"It is. If we leave now, we can be airborne in 90 minutes."

"Then let's go." Replied James. "I've had enough sunshine for now."

Wes and Juddy had reconfigured the seating on the Gulfstream. It was now laid out as a 16-seater passenger jet.

Libby was still sedated and had to be carried aboard. The others, looking at the small jet with something approaching astonishment, chattering, and pointing animatedly. As had been the case with Lyla, this was their first taste of air travel and it was with some difficulty, they were ushered aboard and seated.

James went into the cockpit for a brief chat and soon wished he hadn't.

"Plane fixed then?"

"Nothing to worry about." Wes answered. "We had a few warning lights on. All sorted old lad."

Juddy stared up balefully at James.

"He took the bulbs out. We're all going to die."

James left quickly, hoping this was pilot humour and knowing that both men had mortgages and every intention of getting their aircraft and passengers home in one piece. Everyone was strapped in, the aircraft accelerated, rotated, and headed for England.

Sacha and Christian

Home felt good, less alien, and whole. On landing back at Themis, they felt it unwise to let the girls see too much of the site so dropping Tom, Sacha, and Lyla off, Bailey and the guys, in a brand new minibus, headed north, to a haven set up by a former policewoman for girls such as these.

Sacha was rummaging in the kitchen, looking for breakfast when she was surprised by the arrival of Peter Christian. He knocked, somewhat timidly.

"Mrs. Hood?"

Sacha turned, her hand clutching a jar of instant coffee.

"Mr. Christian." She replied, startled not just at the interruption but by the fact it was him. She'd only ever seen him from an elevated distance, standing in his penthouse window. This was her first contact with the man who had changed their lives, for bad, then good.

"If you like your coffee, I'm hopeful I can offer you something a little more palatable."

The chance of decent coffee aside, this was an encounter Sacha had been seeking for a long time now. She knew that almost everything that had occurred or been built since Ellen's murder, was due to his sense of guilt and a need for forgiveness. Without his seeming need to atone, The Twins would still be roaming free, the girls they'd just released would still be in thrall, and much else besides. She's decided long ago that she held no animosity towards Christian but wasn't entirely sure how much absolution she could offer.

The ride in the elevator was undertaken in the kind of silence usual amongst strangers thrust together in an enclosed space. When the door hissed open, he stood back with a gentlemanly gesture, indicating she should go first. She walked steadily out and into Christian's comfort zone. He offered her a seat on an imposing Chesterfield.

He bustled, a voice from the kitchenette. "I have Columbian Andean, a fine arabica, an exotic Kenyan, Jamaican Blue, and Indonesian Kopi Luwak, you may know it as Civet coffee."

Sacha had heard of none of them bar the Indonesian, produced from undigested grounds excreted by the Civet cat. She was not an exotic coffee girl; preferring it simple, fresh ground and black, but hadn't the heart to say so. He was patently hoping to please her but had fallen victim to the typecasting of Americans when it comes to coffee.

She looked up, he was standing with a pack of coffee in each hand.

"Whatever your favourite is, as long as it's black."

He smiled and turned, chatting earnestly as he went through the grinding process.

"That would be the Jamaican Blue, then. Grown in volcanic soil at altitude and every single bean hand-picked. Most of it goes to Japan, I'm grateful I can get some from source."

Sacha heard the grinder stop, then boiling water pour. A sweet, herbal fragrance perfumed the room and she found herself anticipating the beverage more than the conversation. When it came, she was surprised to see him bearing mugs rather than the fine china rattling on a saucer she'd supposed he'd favour. It was a design she recognised.

"Le Creuset?"

He nodded, handing her the orange stoneware.

"A very effective insulator. When working, I can occasionally forget that the coffee is there. The Le Creuset keeps it hotter for longer."

She held the mug to her nose and breathed in. She was no connoisseur and was startled by her sudden ability to detect subtle accents and tints. The herbal sweetness she'd originally experienced was suffused with floral notes and nutty undertones. She sipped. No bitterness, just a creamy, chocolate sensation. She'd never tasted anything quite like it.

"Wow."

He beamed, grateful that he'd pleased her.

"I shall have some sent over, if you like."

"I do like. That would be immense. Thank you."

They sat quietly, both, for different reasons, savouring the moment. Christian broke the silence.

"Mrs. Hood, or may I call you Sacha?"

She nodded, aware that this would very likely be a difficult conversation for both of them.

"Thank you. I don't know where to begin. I know I've been remiss, that it's been such a long time since the event but perhaps I should first say how terribly sorry I was for what happened to your daughter."

"You can say her name, it was Ellen."

"Yes, I know. I'm sorry. Ellen, of course."

Sacha leaned forward. She knew where responsibility lay for the death of her only child, and, in any way you wanted to look at it, the price for that had been paid. She'd wanted to meet Christian for this express purpose. No-one can anticipate the tread of life, which path people choose to follow, and she knew from her chats with Ames that this man had not intended harm, probably never had. By giving him absolution, she could close down that sad chapter, his guilt the last remaining side effect of the actions of his one-time family. It was time to let go.

"No one blames you, Mr. Christian. Not me, not Tom, no-one. You can take off the hair shirt, stop beating yourself up."

She saw tears well up in his eyes, a faraway expression take over.

"I never believed they could…"

"I know. Let it go. It's ok."

Taking a moment to sip from his mug, Christian regained some composure.

"Are you sure? There's nothing I can…"

"I'm sure. Ellen's resting easy and you gave us, Tom 'n me, a reason to remember what we were. Without Ellen, our lives were always going to be different, empty perhaps and no-one's dumb enough to say Ellen can ever be replaced, but you've earned forgiveness. Perhaps one day, we may even be friends."

Christian welled up a second time. Astonished at the level of emotional maturity this woman displayed. He been seeking forgiveness for himself, when first approaching Tom Hood in that hotel. He'd never expected compassion, perhaps never really understood what it was at a molecular level, but now, he believed that he had some grasp and felt release. There was no longer any need to hide.

"Thank you. From the bottom of my heart. Thank you."

They sat together, finishing the coffee, each waiting for another subject to fill the void. Sacha put down her mug.

"This place, the estate, it's amazing."

"Thank you," then, enthused,

"I bought it for a simple purpose you know, but now, with the people that inhabit it, it seems to have taken on a life of its own. I've grown to appreciate it for more than the sum of its parts, perhaps even to believe it has a soul."

"I do believe you're right, Mr. Christian."

He reached out. "Peter, please call me Peter."

"Ok." She agreed, a deal already done from within.

"I get what you mean, Peter. It just seems to have a beating heart, more than land, bricks and mortar, a place with a gentle purpose, though not always achieved with kid gloves."

Christian nodded. "Do you believe we are breaking the law here? Or at least, the spirit of the law."

"I'm certain of the first part but only because the law seems never likely to be fixed, as for the spirit of the law, we're only fighting fire with fire, there's an edge to the people here that says enough is enough, but the best part is, it's targeted. To my knowledge not a single innocent person has been harmed in anything that gets done in our name, quite the opposite, in fact."

"I'm so very pleased to hear you say that. I wasn't sure what I thought I was doing when I first set the wheels in motion. But doing nothing seemed worse."

"Peter, Ames, Bailey, and the guys, they're the best, they have an internal setting that comes from a good place. I think now, it's time for me 'n Tom to take Lyla home."

Sacha was surprised by the next words.

"Would you bring her here, to see me. I'd be grateful."

"Well, yeah. I guess so, but wouldn't it be better if you came down, just to say Hi?"

Christian seemed immediately unsettled by the proposal. Sacha moved in for the kill.

"You need to get out, Peter. At least from these rooms. You might surprise yourself."

He thought briefly, then appeared to have reached some internal accord with himself. His self-imposed exile had been comforting, at first. But the loneliness he felt as time went on had become wearing, depressing, enlivened until now, only by the occasional visits from Ames. He'd been in hiding, he realised.

"Right. Yes. Perhaps I might."

Washing Up

The site was functional but slightly discouraging. There were signs that money was tight. It was an old schoolhouse, now refunctioned as a residential home.

Ames left his car and entered by the large, blue, solid timber double doors, reminiscent of pre-war architecture. He stood in an enclosed vestibule, eyeing signs and buttons, a security system which he bypassed by speaking his name and purpose. Once through, he entered an office and greeted a deskbound lady. Sandra, he supposed, from their telephone conversations. She was ex-job, like him, but had resigned from the force solely for the purpose of rescuing girls from grooming and trafficking and aiding their recovery from the experience.

"You're expecting us?"

She'd already stood and was threading her way around the desk, hand outstretched. "Yes. Hello. Are they here?"

He inclined his head. "In the minibus. Just sorting out their bits and pieces. By the way, you can keep the bus."

"Oh. Ok. Right, well…Thank you. Can I ask why?"

"It's just a gift," shrugged Ames. "So is this."

He handed her a cheque, drawn on Themis.

Her initial surprise gave way to shock when she saw the numbers.

"Are you for real?"

"Just trying to help." Ames replied.

"There are things you need to know about these girls, though."

Sandra pre-empted his next words with some of her own, practised, and practical.

"We know the kind of problems these girls have, Mr. Ames. And we have the systems in place to deal with them. Drug dependence, low self-esteem, a lack of education, family issues to name a few. This cheque will go a long way towards achieving our aims. We're very grateful."

"Erm. It's not that." Began Ames.

"They may have a story to tell you, one that perhaps will need some discretion on your part."

Sandra looked up from the cheque, still astonished at the number of zeros. "Go on."

"In short, they were being held in Turkey. They'd been trafficked there following years of abuse here in the U.K. We heard about them, got them out."

She cocked an eyebrow, well versed in trafficking routes and disappearances.

"Got them out?"

"Well, that's it, really. Nothing more to tell."

Sandra let that go, the girls would be more forthcoming.

"Shall we go outside, get the girls in and settled?"

She led the way, curious to see what she'd find. In the car park, was a shiny minibus and two cars. There were 8 girls, as expected, most looking remarkably fit and tanned for trafficking victims. Just one stood separate from the group, a haunted, hunted expression on her face. Sandra knew that look well, bitter experience telling her that some recoveries took longer than others. Time didn't necessarily heal all things.

Around them, she noted their escorts consisted of four men and a woman, and she knew enough from past experience in the job, that they weren't from the Salvation Army, but most likely former members of another one.

Ames stood beside her. "If you send us the bills for day to day running, electricity, maintenance and the like, we'll take care of them for the foreseeable future."

Sandra took the card he offered. Themis, she noted. *'Never heard of them.'*

"Is this the price for my discretion?"

"No." Replied Ames. "That's not how we work."

"How do you work?"

A tall man handed her the keys to the minibus, then joined his companions as they took their seats in the cars.

"Quietly." Said Ames. Then fired up the car, leading the group out onto the road and heading south.

Ames looked at the number. It was a call he'd been anticipating. Arham. Adjusting his mindset, he took it.

"Arham. Good morning."

"Morning, Stuart." There was a pause. Ames waited, letting his former colleague set the agenda.

"So, I've had a surprisingly good month."

"You have?"

"You'll recall sending me an address a while back?"

"I had information I thought you ought to know. I didn't know where it might lead. All work out, did it?" Replied Ames.

"You could say that."

"I'm pleased to hear it. You never know where these whispers might lead."

Ames was waiting for the thrust of the conversation to emerge, as it knew it surely would.

"Where did the information come from?"

"Confidential source." Ames answered. "Does it matter?"

"If you can't tell me," Said Arham, knowing that can't or won't are much the same thing, "Then it's academic."

"Fine." Said Ames. "So, did it pan out?"

Arham chuckled. "You could say that. When we got there, the front door was wide open, and apparently unoccupied so we were able to legally enter, Section 17, save life, limb, property, and all that stuff. Guess what we found?"

"Pretty much what I said you would." Replied Ames. "Some underage girls being mistreated."

"Well there was that, and thank you, but there was more, so much more."

Arham's glee was undisguised. "Some girls in shit state, caged in the cellar. We got them out and they're in care now and ok, but upstairs, oh the joy of what we found upstairs."

"Go on."

"Only our very own PCC, off his tits on coke and surrounded by videos, photos, USB's full of the vilest crap involving young girls and starring him and his mates."

"Double whammy, then." Ames offered, his tone upbeat, as if surprised by the discovery.

"And then some, but it gets better. From that footage, we've ID'd literally dozens of these fuckers. Businessmen, builders, taxi drivers, they were all at it. Our cells are full and all those useless twats that were interfering or ignoring goings on, suddenly are either running for the hills or keeping their heads down. Not a single, fucking word about racism from the PC brigade. Some big reputations are in tatters, policies are being revised, resignations offered and accepted. Some of that stuff is on VHS! Going back years. We're actually catching criminals, mate."

The story was tumbling from Arham. Ames let him continue.

"D'you know girls from way back are coming forward. The ones that were labelled pathetic liars, now, at last, being taken seriously. Social services are falling over themselves; lawyers are in short supply for our poor, persecuted perverts, and I'm in copper heaven. Morale is sky high here. My people are working overtime and not claiming it. Stuart, it's a massive hit."

Ames waited, despite Arham's obvious elation, he knew he'd have questions.

"Well if I hear anything else, I'll let you know."

"Hold up, Stuart." Arham paused. "I'm grateful for the info but curious that after years of being fucked over, I have a little moan to you…you remember that call?"

Ames assented that he did.

"Well, it didn't take long for things to start happening, did it? One call to you and my world turned. How?"

Ames was ready for this. "Coincidence."

"Right. Wasn't it Einstein who said that coincidence is God's way of remaining anonymous?"

Ames gave his answer some consideration. God's way. Themis, in this instance. But he couldn't say that.

'Goes against the creed.' He thought, smiling. Then replied,

Who's Einstein?"

There was a pause on the line. He was being deliberately disingenuous, and Arham knew it.

"Right. And if I should ever need to make another social call?"

"Then you have my number, Arham."

Ames closed the call, his mind on what to do next. This, their first, real operation, had concluded satisfactorily but experience told him that there was always something, always someone that needed to be stopped. He felt content that these past weeks had justified his initial, shaky faith in Themis. The world would throw up another task, of that he was certain, he would work to see that Themis was ready for it. First though, he would grab a bottle of malt and three glasses.

Home

"The boys'll be here for Christmas, work allowing."

Sacha had just come off the phone, keen to hear how the handover had worked out.

"The girls are where they should be, getting the help they'll need."

"Cool," replied Tom. "But have you seen what Inga's done?"

Sacha had. The copse cemetery now had dreamcatchers and 'thought' memorials in abundance.

"Can't wait for the winter solstice." Tom grumbled. "Druids and Celts wandering all over the place, mumbling and sticking pins in dolls."

"It'll be effigies of you they'll be sticking pins in. Don't be such a sourpuss, Tom Hood. I think it's fun."

On arriving home, their near month's absence had been greeted in the first instance, by Pooh. Who had an interest in all that took place and was enthusiastic about being the first to know. In the tv room, some tail wagging from the older dogs made them feel at home and the kitchen meeting that morning had been filled with conversation.

"You lot look well." Said Donna, taking in the tans. "Been somewhere nice?"

"Turkey!" Lyla had replied, aware that that was as much as should be said. Then carried on about the lovely villa, the pool, the weather.

Lyla's new teacher, Yvette, who Tom, and Sacha had not yet met was now a fixture. Helping out with the kennels when not busy preparing for her new role. While waiting for her new pupil she'd prepared a room and set it out as a classroom. The tone needed to be right, she'd said.

"You don't sound French." Tom stated, remembering how she'd been proposed by Donna and Inga.

"On my grandfather's side. Those two do exaggerate."

"A bit tenuous, isn't it?" Replied Tom.

"No more so than your claim to be English, Mr. Hood. Your surname is relating to or denoting Germanic inhabitants arriving in England from the 5th century up to the Norman conquest."

"That told him." Said Inga, smiling at Tom's perplexed expression.

"Puffin's egg for breakfast, Inga?"

"Fook off, Tom.

Sacha was in the kitchen, thinking briefly of what lay beneath her feet. The cellar where a few years back, Tom had begun his quest for revenge. Covered over and disused now that they had the estate and all that came with it; it was still their genesis, the beginning of everything when all else had died with Ellen. At the thought of her daughter, Sacha climbed the stairs.

She found Lyla in her room, unpacking, and sorting her laundry.

"Well honey, that was some adventure."

Lyla shifted the conversation, there was something on her mind.

"That Mr. Christian was nice."

Lyla had a way of weaving conversations that combined the past with the present. Sacha had to think for a moment then remembered being back at the estate on that last day, watching as Christian and Lyla had taken a walk together outside. On their return, Lyla seemed incredulous that though everything around them was his, Christian didn't seem to know any of it, apparently having lived upstairs for ever. For a girl who was used to nothing, she couldn't understand why all he owned seemed to mean so little.

"That'll change, honey." Sacha had replied, confident that Peter would now climb down from his battlements.

Lyla had paused then, gazing intently at Sacha, finding the words she very much needed to say.

"We're staying here now, right?"

"Yep. You're gonna get an education, we're all gonna have a life."

"Will you ever have to go away again, you and Tom, on your own?"

Sacha knew that that meant, *'without me.'* She knew then what was on the young girls' mind and tried to find a way of settling it, without making any promises she couldn't keep.

"Can't never say never, honey. There's stuff going on out there that can't be left. If we're asked, we'll go. But we'll always come back. And there's the ladies and Sid, while we're gone. This is your home. It'll always be your home."

Lyla remembered her old home, her old life, the despair, the wretchedness, and hopelessness of it all, the rapes, the beatings, the awful dread of it, never ending, day after day. It was stuff she wanted to forget, to never remember again. She thought of the pictures of the little girl on the wall, Ellen, who'd been so very pretty and couldn't imagine the sadness of it, of her not being here. So she would remember the little girl she'd never known and in that way, forget the girl she'd been forced to be. She knew she was going to cry but didn't want Sacha to see it, didn't want her think she was sad. Lyla stood up from her clothes folding, dropped what was in her hands onto the bed and almost stumbling in her haste, rushed across the room, into Sacha's arms. She held on tight and was held with the same devotion in kind.

"I love you, Sacha."

Tears sprung to her eyes and Sacha felt something inside her swell. She could barely speak from the strength of it.

"I love you too, honey. I love you too."

Authors Note

'We Were Swans' Was intended to be the first and last book we would write. It began as an exercise, a retirement project, something to do. This book, 'Tell Me There's a Reason' was written because we were asked for it. Our problem now is that Sacha, Tom, Lyla, and all at Themis are family now, and we like having them around.

Themis will be back.

Printed in Great Britain
by Amazon